'A heath of wild and frightful aspect with groves, thickets and forest; and a fit refuge for all manner of vagabonds, cut-throat tinkers, footpads and highwaymen.'

This was Roehampton in 1798 according to a clerk giving instructions to Jeremy Sturrock, Bow Street Runner, sent there to investigate a crime.

An historical crime novel set solidly in the eighteenth century is something different, especially if its form is that of a classical puzzle whodunnit. Here the action is fast and furious as well: because Jeremy Sturrock, although a man of nice gentility – especially with the ladies – is uncommonly useful with his fists in a good sporting mill, and by no means slow with his pistols when the need arises.

Being, as he styles himself, a master in the new Art and Science of Detection, he has no difficulty in probing the tangle of characters and motives that surround the sudden violent death of Lord Hartingfield. And in this he is aided by the youthful, crafty and bloodthirsty wretch Maggsy whom he quickly acquires as personal aide and occasional spy.

This action-packed whodunnit has many humorous touches, and some witty comment. Despite its pace and its mystery and its horrific occurrences, this is a highly civilised debut by Jeremy Sturrock, which pseudonym cloaks the name of an established crime writer who has never previously written an historical mystery.

JEREMY STURROCK

The Village of Rogues

MACMILLAN

SBN Boards: 333 13337 4

First published 1972 by
MACMILLAN LONDON LTD
London and Basingstoke
Associated companies in New York Toronto
Dublin Melbourne Johannesburg & Madras

Printed in Great Britain by
RICHARD CLAY (THE CHAUCER PRESS), LTD
Bungay, Suffolk

Author's Note

All characters in this book are entirely fictitious; although some people may feel that Roehampton itself has not changed very much.

I

'A heath of wild and frightful aspect with groves, thickets and forest; and a fit refuge for all manner of vagabonds, cut-throat tinkers, footpads and highwaymen. There are several low taverns and alehouses, one such being close by the new telegraph signal on the Portsmouth Road, and the King's Head at the hamlet of Roehampton; the first are rude places much frequented by drovers, the lower sort of mariners, and some smugglers, while the other is said to be of good livery and bait with lodging for six or more travellers. Apart from certain mansions to the west side of Putney Hill you have at Roehamptom, and abutting on the aforesaid heath, the estates of my Lord Hartingfield – whom this robbery and purloinage concerns; or, to be the more precise, my Lady Hartingfield – and of Sir Tobias Westleigh; who, though Justice of the Peace for this parish, is reputed a notorious rake, womaniser, gambler and, in general, sportsman.' That was the direction which my master's clerk had written for me; a good fellow, but somewhat over inclined to take up his pen with a Gothick flourish.

Myself I am a man of few and blunt words, so I'd best make myself known and have done with it. Jeremy Sturrock of the Bow Street Runners and, saving my proper modesty, the best of the lot; a notable thief taker, and an honest man. A biggish figure, but not corpulent, wearing decent sober clothes – though not without a certain elegance in my style – and a benevolent manner except when dealing with rogues, villains, and those of the lower sort who need to be reminded of their place. Of fresh complexion and hopeful nature barring a variable touch of liver in the mornings; also a very fair pugilist and, when the need arises, sharp with my pistols. As to age, that's my business; but I can still rollick a ready wench, and often do when matters of the law spare me the time.

I am a man risen from nothing to my present eminence; my old father being a costermonger, middling honest, but not all that much in his head. For my part I perceived while young that for the simpler kind the only roads out of Spittalfields were by way of the pox, the cholera or a hemp necklace, and for none of which did I have much fancy so I took up with a family of silk weavers and set about learning my letters and figuring with an old screever. This, for the benefit of the genteel, is a rogue who makes his trade writing pitiful proclamations for beggars, noble epistles such as can be used to work a con, testimonials for rascally servants, and so forth; and is a sure way of learning a very persuasive style of the noble English language.

These silk weavers being poor but proper people I was cast out on the street again with a boot in my arse, when the youngest daughter set about improving my education under the table one night. The cold was bitter that winter and by Divine Guidance I found my way into the Courts of the Assize to keep warm, and for the moral example of watching the judgements. There I learned the wickedness of human nature, especially among the lower sort, and the majesty of the law; and there also I fell in with a sodden old lawyer's clerk who was taken sober with amazement by my lettering and reading; so I now turned to doing his scribing when he

8

was too far gone to hold a quill and it began to be made plain to me that I was marked out by a Wise and All Seeing Providence for special favour. Whereon I took to attending Holy Service on Sundays, within reason and to make sure of the matter, and when old Ebenezer died of a drunken flux – they say his nose bled gin at the last – it was this same Providence, to the end of putting down rogues and villains, which led me to the Bow Street Office there to enlist in the Runners. As you might expect I did well for myself, and by 1786 I was appointed to a special honour as one of the two bodyguards to His Majesty King George III; God bless him, as he was most need of blessing in his affliction and troubles, poor soul.

Thus I learned a nice gentility, and I am not bashful to say that there are few who have come so far from such vulgar beginnings. Indeed there is none at all who is my master or my equal in this new profession of what I shall call Detection; which is the art and science of tracking down and apprehending your felon, malefactor or criminal by the use of observations, considerations and philosophical logic. Scarcely known of yet, it is a study which will be sorely needed in time to come if we are to stem the flood of villainy which is rising about us in this land; and I often consider that before some rogue ends me with the knife or a pistol shot I should do well to set down a short treatise or exposition of it for the instruction of others. It pleases me to think even that I might plead the interest of His Majesty, for I hold it a highly genteel thing to have a Royal name on the first page of your book. But that is not for the present work; this being a mere light tale, though not without certain moral reflections, which will serve to wile away an idle hour

9

and perhaps give some small entertainment to the ladies, whom I always strive to please.

So you are to see me on this dark afternoon, the eighteenth day of December 1798, being borne creaking and swaying up Putney Hill in a hired chaise. Properly the Bow Street Runners are expected to take horse when called out of town, and there is always a pair waiting; but for my part I cannot abide the beasts – no man can excel at everything – and I consider, moreover, that the law should move in dignity. So I am sitting with my feet in a lock of straw for comfort, my capes pulled about me and a brace of holster pistols lying ready in case of need. The dark is thickening early and the road not as bad as many but foul enough; the high wall of some estate to one side, the gateposts to gentlemen's residences on the other and a whiffle of snow falling. The post boy is crouching with his head into the wind, and I can tell by the cut of him that the surly rogue is blaspheming his heart out; they are all the same, these coachmen, horse boys and ostlers.

We pass a pot house with the swinging sign of a Green Man; a miserable place, but with a gleam of light in its windows and a rag of smoke from the chimney. To the other hand there is the beginning of a wild waste, doubtless the Putney Heath of which Abel Makepenny had written in my directions; and from what you could see with the snow settling about its dark thickets, it looked fit to harbour scores of villains who'd be the better of a good hanging. It was more than likely the particular fellow I was after myself would be lurking in there now, but I resolved not to enter that place without especial care. I think little enough of the rookeries – where a wise man goes with a stout cudgel, one hand to his pistol, and eyes in his arse – but I am no fool, for these countrymen are well known to be cunning and savage rascals.

My boy had much the same thoughts, for he set to peering sideways over his shoulder and broke the horses into a rough trot while I made the observations, as a sea captain crony of mine has it, and loosened my pistols in their holsters. For a long mile or more we rattled through that pestilential heath and then took to swinging and clattering down another little hill between a huddle of cottages; a damned rough ride, bouncing about like an apple in a chamber pot, and I cursed that young rogue's soul to hell, swearing I'd have the skin off his shoulders if ever I came safe out of it. Yet such is the kindness of my nature that no sooner had we swung round at last into a cobbled yard and he dismounted and opened the door to me, seeing the stabling and the lamps lit, than I said, 'You can take a quart of mulled ale at my charge,' making sure as I spoke that it would be more than one quart or two. These post boys are prodigious drinkers and pissers.

It was a fair house, decently clapboarded and prosperous by the look of it, with good wide bays and firelight shining in them through the snow. There was a comical painted likeness of a comfortable old drinker, with a big belly and a pot in one hand and his pipe in the other, on the inner door; and the landlord himself was not unlike this amiable rascal, save that he'd got a red stuff weskit and a breath of brandy wine about him when he spoke. 'Well met, sir; welcome to the King's Head. You'll be lodging?' he asked. 'Then there's a snug chamber with the fire already lit. Likewise we're just about to serve up to another gentleman in the parlour; a nice sirloin, a brace of

11

capons and a fine venison pie this minute out of the oven.' And like enough not long out of the Royal Park of Richmond; but I thought His Majesty wouldn't begrudge me a bite of one of his deer.

It was a fine commodious room, very comfortable after that damnable dark heath and the snow, with excellent polished panelling, candles already lit and a good log fire blazing; and the other gentleman taking his ease by it, with a pot of mulled claret ready on the hearth stone, having thrown off his riding boots the better to toast his feet at the blaze. Thirtyish or a year or so more, with a weathered colour to his face; dressed to the mode yet by no means foppish, hair in the country style, a hard chin, and a don't give a damn for man or devil look about him. But he said civilly, 'A foul night, sir. Have you travelled far?'

'Far enough,' I answered. 'From London. In a pestilential draughty post chaise. And a surly, disobliging rogue of a boy to suit.'

'They're all the same, these fellows,' he observed. 'We live in unmannerly days, and growing worse. Did you have any trouble with our famous Knights of the Highway while crossing the heath?'

'Now, sir,' I admonished him warmly, 'let us have no such talk of these rascals being famous. To raise them to the dignity of Knighthood, sir, places them on a level with our gentry, which I will not admit. And the pretence of their courtesies to the ladies, if you believe the vulgar talk, are no more than mere tales of ostlers and the ale house wenches whom they rollick in the hay between their crimes. Depend upon it, there's never a one of these villains who wouldn't be the handsomer of his neck stretching by an inch or more.'

'You speak with heat,' he said. 'Have you suffered at

their hands, then?'

'Not so much as they've suffered at mine,' I answered with some satisfaction. 'And I'll go so far to add that, until the roads of this kingdom are safe for any innocent traveller to go abroad on, the best sight any honest man can see is a good gallows, well constructed and in regular use. I was remarking as much to the King himself only a few weeks since and His Majesty, God bless him, although a merciful man was graciously pleased to agree.' Now here is a moral observation which you should note; that however excellent the company you find yourself in there is never any harm in letting it be known, but always with exact gentility, that you are well accustomed to better.

He was plainly impressed, considering me shrewdly while I settled myself in the other armchair against the fire; then he said, 'Permit me to introduce myself, sir; Tobias Westleigh, Justice of this parish.' At this I pushed myself up again and bowed, saying, 'Your servant, sir; Jeremy Sturrock, of Bow Street,' and he continued, 'Dare one hazard a guess that you are here on the matter of my Lady Hartingfield's jewels?'

'The same, Sir Tobias,' I answered. 'As the nobility, gentry and commonality are requested to do in their own interest, my Lord Hartingfield wrote an account of the affair to Bow Street. I have been sent in answer to his complaint.'

'You're late,' he said. 'It's two days since. You've let the scent run cold.'

'By the art of detection, sir, no scent is ever cold.'

But he shook his head at that. 'Depend upon it, the fellow's in London now.'

'We have our own intelligences,' I told him. 'And I'm persuaded that the villain is still lurking hereabouts. There's cover enough for him. One Thomas Godsave. A countryman, as I understand?'

'From Essex. Brought up here a year back, as second groom.'

'And you know the value of my Lady's jewels?'

'Near enough thirty thousand, so I'm told.'

'A very tidy parcel. Consider, sir,' I said warmly, 'a countryman, a simple fellow with that kind of merchandise about him. Why, then, if he fled to the rookeries they'd skin him overnight and pick his bones clean by morning.'

'Unless he had the matter already arranged. An accomplice.'

'They'd still skin him. And how would a countryman from Essex get himself such an accomplice?' Our people came in to set the table then; the landlord, a serving man, and a pretty pert buxom wench who gazed at me with some interest, and I took the occasion to order a quart of mulled claret, begging Sir Tobias to do me the honour of sharing it. That attended to I continued, 'I'd be obliged, sir, if you'd tell me what you've heard about the matter.'

'Little enough,' he admitted. 'Merely that my Lady Hartingfield is driving back from Alton in her coach and Godsave steps out from the thicket across Cut Throat Lane and cries "Stand and deliver".'

'About five of the evening, we're informed. So it was well dark. And who identified this Godsave? Her ladyship? The coachman; the groom or the footman?'

'The coachman; her ladyship was too affrighted. There was no groom; nor footman. Hartingfield,' Sir Tobias observed, 'keeps a reduced establishment. The man's a skinflint; somewhat elderly and professed of poor health.'

'And my lady herself?' I asked. 'What manner of person is she?'

'French,' he answered shortly, 'not above twenty-eight. She escaped from Paris in '92; before the Terror.'

I will confess I spoke out of turn then, with a shade less than my habitual delicacy, but no more than any other true Englishman can I put up with Frenchies and I cried out, 'Here's a fine kettle of fish. A skinflint lord, a country clod highwayman and a Frenchy.'

For an instant Sir Tobias stared at me with a damnation cold look about his eyes and his cheeks turning paler under the claret flush. Of a certainty at that moment I was close to sudden mischief – with all my experience I've learned to smell it by now – but then he leaned forward to push a log deeper into the fire with the nicest care. In a voice as soft as silk he said, 'Sir, as a stranger among us I would wish to receive you with courtesy. But you'll permit me to announce that if I hear such similar derogation of my lady from your lips again I shall give myself the privilege of breaking your blasted neck, Bow Street Runner or not.'

So you will observe that already I had discovered how the matter lay in that direction, but unwilling to be outdone in the genteel I answered, 'Sir, if you feel an itch to break my neck you are welcome to try, though you might not find it such an easy joint to crack. Apart from that, as from one gentleman to another, if I have spoken to give offence I ask your pardon. And I will concede that if my Lady Harting-field left France before those bloodthirsty savages murdered their own anointed king I was impolite. Yet, mark me, these rascals'll cost us dear before we've done with 'em; them and their damned Bonaparte. As you may see already in Mr. Pitt's most recent invention of Income Tax.'

He continued to regard me with that stare of his before he gave a laugh damned near as hard and said, 'There's one thing you may be sure of; Lady Hartingfield's no Jacobin. And for the rest, let it pass. To cement that, I'll take a glass of claret with you.' It was handsomely done, in a fine stylish manner; and, peace being restored, he asked, 'When d'you propose to set about hunting this Godsave? And if one may ask, what do you make of the whole matter?'

'For the first,' I answered, 'you'll need a fine lantern to seek out a highwayman on a night like this. My method has ever been philosophical consideration, and it ever will be. For the second, and in short, I will observe that the story as I see it this far has as many holes in it as a rabbit may escape from a warren.'

That amused him heartily, but there was no more said then, for they were bringing in the sirloin, capons and venison pie, and we drew up at the table and fell to; myself most willingly, being more than sharp set after my long journey. Yet there was food for thought here also and I was not too busy to put my thinking cap on, this being a headgear which is never far from my hand. Nevertheless, we made a very fair meal – apart from the servers and that buxom wench coming in and out, bringing a draught with 'em – and took another quart of mulled claret between us, while the snow fell steadily beyond the window, the firelight flickered on the panelling of the chamber, and we continued to discourse on the ways and manners of roguery.

I was loosening my waistband and contemplating another assault on the pie when there was a sort of whining, squeaking little voice from beneath the very table, and something plucking at my knee like a dog. 'What have we here?' I asked, and looked down to see the raggedest little bundle you ever set eyes on, a bunch of tow hair, two eyes like a jack-daw peering at me and a mouthful of uncommonly white teeth. Being well on to benevolent then I repeated, 'What have we here?' and reached out to the mop of hair to lift it up.

It was a small boy or urchin, not much higher than your elbow; a pitiful scarecrow. Bare foot, his tail and knees sticking out of his breeches and no more than the rag of a shirt, as black as the devil's whiskers and blue with chill where he wasn't black. He squeaked, 'Give us a mouthful to eat, guv'nor. I'm starving of the cold. I'll do a cartwheel, stand on my head, anything you fancy.'

Sir Tobias let out a great laugh, and I was bound to echo it myself; but I gave the horrible little mannikin a shake by the hair and said, 'How did you come here then? Was it down the chimney? Begod, you'll have got your cobblers singed if you did.'

At which the server came in and bawled, 'So there you be. Crept in while the door was open. I'll flay you for this. Let me have the little whelp, your worship.'

'Let be,' I told him, holding the object up the better to observe it. 'What's your name?' I asked.

'Maggsy,' he whined, 'as near as I know.'

'Chimney sweeper's boy,' I observed. 'And for certain a thieving pilfering rascal like all the tribe.'

'I never was,' he screamed. 'You get your neck cricked for that and I wouldn't do it. Mr. William Makepeace, the Practical Chimney Sweep, beat me wicked, but I still wouldn't do it so I run away.'

The server spoke up again. 'Been skulking about the stables this three days, sleeping with the arses; give me the little bleeder . . .' and I told him, 'I said to let be; and have care to your language.' The tale was likely enough true; these chimney boys are notorious light-fingered imps, trained to it by their owners who turn them away when they grow too big to work, so they starve and fidget from one villainy to another and finish with transportation or on the gallows.

I considered; and I'll not pretend it wasn't the mulled claret and a full belly that was doing my thinking for me. But it had long been a fancy of mine to have myself a private clerk or amanuensis – a most elegantly genteel thing in my view – to set down my moral observations as I let them fall, and to record my reflections and instructions on the Art and Science of Detection. And here he was ready to my hand at a cost of no more than a few pence a week. True, he was a poor toad; but under the loving Hand of our Lord there is none so rough that he may not be modelled if taken young and cuffed hard and often enough. I said, 'Can you read and letter?'

The rascal had spirit enough to sneer at me. 'What d'you take me for? They don't have no colleges in Seven Dials.'

Giving him a smack across the head for a first lesson I said, 'You'll mind your pertness for a start,' while Sir Tobias watched me with a quizzical look in his eye, for many people would have had the child out to the stable yard and a whipping by now. That made up my mind for me and I added, 'He stinks of soot and dung. Have him outside and dowse him in the horse trough to sweeten him.'

Sir Tobias let out another laugh at that, but the

little oddikin screeched, 'Lord Jesus it'll be me death,' and I gave him another cuff, saying, 'And you'll watch your blasphemous tongue,' and then, seeing the lowering grin on that serving man's face, I added, 'See it's no more than a dowsing. If you go beyond that I'll put my cane about your shoulders.'

'Begod, here's a diversion,' Sir Tobias observed, 'and with your permission, sir, I'll take a hand in it myself. We've a brat near enough his size running about the House at this present; some nephew of my housekeeper's and she's a good charitable woman.' The child set up another screech and he barked, 'Go to it, boy; it's high time you was baptised by the look of you,' and turned to the man. 'You'll find my groom, Trimmer, in the tap. Have him ride up to the House and beg an outfit of Master Edward's clothes from Mrs. Peggit; smalls, pantaloons, everything he needs. And you can throw those filthy rags aside and wrap him in a horse blanket until they arrive.'

It is well known the gentry are liable to their sudden whims, and I am never the man to look a gift horse in the teeth. I answered, 'You're most kind, sir; and a generous action is never lost sight of at the Last Reckoning.' So, screeching that he hadn't counted on cold water and he'd as soon starve and do without it, the stinking little rogue was dragged out while I addressed myself again to His Majesty's venison pie. And then we listened to a dismal hooting and yellocking, like a little pig, amid howls of vulgar laughter from the stable yard. 'God's faith,' Sir Tobias said, 'it sounds as if they're gutting him.'

But you could see he was curious to know what I wanted the boy for, and lest he should entertain any lewd and fanciful notions on the matter I told him plainly. 'You must understand that I am in need of a servant and clerk. But fully grown they come expensive, as well as often being rascals, and I fancy that this brat, properly trained, might suit very well. He's of an age to learn fast from a touch of the cane behind and a full belly in front. To put it short, I shall secure the creature for a modicum and mould him as I will. To say nothing of most likely saving his neck.'

There was still a damned quizzical look in his eye but he murmured, 'A clerk? Does one perceive a man of letters?'

'Say rather of science. I am contemplating a treatise or dissertation on the Art and Mystery of what I call Detection, which is the business of tracing, apprehending and confounding your villain or criminal by the application of logic and the consideration of evidence.'

Once again he was vastly impressed, but there was no time to expound more, although on this subject I may talk for hours if need be, because on that the door opened and they brought the boy back. The serving man and a hulking ostler, grinning like a horse for all he had a cut upon his chin and one eye already darkening. 'A rare little wild cat,' he observed. 'Took four of us to hold the bastard down. Had near enough to drown'n in the end.'

It was a woebegone sight. Where he'd been black and blue before he was near enough all blue now; shaking like the ague, teeth chattering in his jaws, his mop head dripping water and his eyes showing the whites of wickedness. A rare clerk he looked, and for a minute I thought of telling them to take him off again with a penny for his pains; but the scamp wriggled himself free, fetched the fellow a smart blow in the belly, and made a rush for the fire; and my natural mercifulness forbade me to turn him away. He was steaming like a drab's clouts, and Sir Tobias gave another of his laughs and tossed the men a coin saying, 'Bathe your wounds with that,' while I busied myself taking a leg of the capon and carving a good fat rib out of the beef. The little rogue snatched them out of my hands, snarling as if he'd like to eat me too, and I cried, 'We'll have to teach you a touch of gentility, my mannikin.'

'You've rough material here,' Sir Tobias said. 'It's natural gallows' meat or I never saw any.'

'We'll save the villain yet,' I answered.

So we left him to sit there gnawing at the bones like a dog, now and again tossing him another until he started to swell under our eyes, while we discoursed genteelly of one thing and another, called for a fresh quart of claret and smoked our pipes. Little more was said of Thomas Godsave and my Lady Hartingfield's jewels, and I was content enough with that, for it suited me better to sit quiet and observe this fine sportsman of a Justice of the Peace; reflecting that there were deep waters here.

It was an hour, and the boy stinking and roasting at the fire, before there was a scratching on the door and Sir Tobias's man appeared. A fellow with a powder of snow on his shoulders and once more a look of the sporting fancy about him, such as you may see by the score on Epsom Downs. He said, 'The clo'es, your honours. Master Edward's third best. And Mrs. Peggit's a thought vexed; she says if it mean another to the house tonight . . .'

Sir Tobias cut him short. 'Begod, no; not at any price. Here, get the scamp into them before he cooks himself alive.'

So with the dint of a few cuffs and some squealing

and cursing, the toad being of a natural rebellious nature, we got him dressed; looking near enough like a little gentleman, except for his ugly face, and smelling sweeter. Then, seeing that Sir Tobias was tiring of the diversion as the gentry often do with their whims, I read the boy a short improving lecture on his duty and manners etc. – for the young should always be sent to bed with certain moral observations to reflect on – and concluded. 'Now you can be off. You're to find the landlord and tell him you're appointed my clerk, and you may sleep in my room; on the hearth. And give thanks to God for His mercies and this gentleman and me. Likewise see that the fire's bright and clean for when I come up; and make sure there's a chamber pot under the bed.' For you must note that some of these inns are careless in that respect, which leads to discomfort.

It was a pert little villain; for on the instant he answered, 'And I wish't I might put some gunpowder in it to singe your cod for that dowsing you gave me.'

There was nothing for it but to fetch him a slap across the chaps which near enough landed him into what was left of the venison pie; and then Trimmer took him by the ear, while Sir Tobias observed indifferently, 'I fear you'll need a whip to that rogue before you've done. Now, sir, let's have them in to clear this away, and settle for a little entertainment. A hand of cards or a song or two? By the look of you you'll have a fine fruity voice.'

I am over cautious with my money to play cards with the gentry – although, as you will have seen, open handed enough in all other respects – and I answered, 'Let it be a song.' So I gave him 'The Fishman's Wife of Billingsgate', which is a laughable romp although somewhat bawdy, and he retorted with 'The Fine Lady of St. James's'; beating time to it I broke my pipe and had to call for another. Then I rendered a sad, comical ballad of Newgate Jail, this being an example for all poor villains who do not see the wickedness of their ways before it gets too late; and he replied again with a scandalous catch concerning Princess Caroline and His Royal Highness the Prince of Wales, upon which I felt constrained to remonstrate although in the genteelest possible manner.

Nevertheless it was all merry enough until he started on the words of a canting doggerel that fetched me up short between my pipe and my wine, and gave me meat for thought; not that a fine gentleman should know such a song, for it was middling respectable against the other on the Princess, but where he should have picked it up. The last time I heard it was in a whore house on the Bermondsey Marshes, bawled in the parlour while in a closet nearby one villain was striving to cut my throat and his doxy doing her best to claw my eyes out – needless to say I had the better of them and later saw the pair hanged for it on a bitter cold morning while I was drinking a pot of hot rum punch. But it was a song I never thought to hear from a Justice of the Peace in the hamlet of Roehampton. This was the way it went.

'My true love she was beautiful, my true love she was
young;
Her eyes was like two diamonds bright
And silv'ry was her tongue.
And silv'ry was her tongue, my lads,
Tho' now she's far away,

*She's taken a trip on a Gov'ment ship ten thousand
    miles away.'*

'Well,' Sir Tobias cried, 'what d'you think of that
one, Mr. Bow Street Runner?'

'Fair enough,' I answered. 'Though I've heard it
before, Sir Tobias. So let's have the chorus, just to
show I know it.'

*'Sing ho, my lads, sing hey, my lads,
Where the dancing dolphins play,
And the whales and sharks are up to their larks
Ten thousand miles away.'*

'Choicely good, sir,' I said. 'Choicely good. A fine
rollicking ditty to retire upon.'

'God's faith, man,' he asked, 'so early? Will you not
make a night of it?'

'I ask your pardon, sir,' I told him. 'Tomorrow I
have heavy work to do. The majesty of the law must be
maintained.'

I rose up somewhat thoughtfully, reflecting that our
excellent Sir Tobias was clearly a man of wide experience. And thinking, perhaps a shade obscure but not
without meaning, that he who eats plums with the
devil must not be surprised if he gets the stones spat in
his eye.

II

Backus, the landlord, was awaiting me in the tap, pretty well aglow with brandy himself. He had a sideways trick of peering at you from the corners of his eyes which I mistrusted, but he enquired civilly enough, 'Good entertainment, your honour?'

'Very fair,' I answered. 'Very fair indeed.'

'You'll take a glass of brandy?' he suggested.

He led me into a little closet or snug, with a trapway or hatch to one side from where he could watch what was going on in the tap, and to the other end a bay window with the darkness beyond and the snow still drifting down. 'A bitter night,' he said, giving me another of his sidelong looks while pouring out the liquor. 'I'd be sorry for any poor soul lying out there.'

'Like this Thomas Godsave?' I asked. 'Well, if he perishes of cold it'll save a rope. But no doubt there's a few shelters where he might lie snug. Maybe with a doxy to keep him warm.'

'Not Tom ...' he started, but then checked himself. 'It's a wild waste, that heath. For my part I never set foot upon it except with a fowling piece and a pair of dogs. We've a fair shoot of mallard and sometimes the chance of a goose.' He appeared to be considering his words, watching me while I savoured the brandy, and then said, 'A word to the wise, Mr. Sturrock; and everybody can see you're that. If you're about the business I fancy you are you'd do well to think about a certain Captain Roderick Medfield.'

'A rare brandy, Mr. Backus,' I answered. 'A most excellent brandy, and getting scarce these days through the trouble with these damnation Frenchies. And who's Captain Roderick Medfield?'

'A right whoring, roaring blade. And the heir to the title but not the property; if you take my meaning.'

'Bedamn,' I said, 'I don't. You talk in mysteries.'

'It's plain enough. Hartingfield's getting on; and sick, or so he fancies. When he goes Captain Roderick'll find himself "my lord"; but my lord without two pence to rub together, for there's no love lost between them.' He stopped and then added, 'Unless it be ...' but cut himself short once more and finished, 'A smell more brandy, Mr. Sturrock?'

'I'll not say no; it's gratifying to the stomach. Unless it be what, Mr. Backus?' But he did not answer that and I continued, 'You're saying this Captain Roderick don't get the property so he's helped himself to a trifle on account; a small matter of thirty thousand?'

One of the candles was guttering and my landlord clipped it with his fingers, a thing I'll confess I'm never so bold to do. 'I'm a man as picks his words.'

'I see you are,' I answered. 'And you pick 'em with a nice delicacy. But so far as my information goes the coachman – what's his name? – swore to Godsave.'

'Buckle,' he observed. 'Depend upon it, that'll be false witness. Him and the captain's as thick as thieves when that fine soldier's hereabouts. The captain reckon's himself a whip, 'tis the fashion these days, and it pays Buckle to indulge him.'

I considered that, finishing my brandy and watching this fellow, wondering what his interest was; but he did not seem inclined to add any more and I said, 'I'm obliged to you, Mr. Backus; you've given me food for thought as well as a drop of very palatable brandy. But for now I'll go to find this snug chamber you promised.'

'I'll light you up myself,' he offered.

The boy was sleeping on the hearth like a dog, and when I stirred him with my toe he came round like one too, until he saw who it was; for the minute I thought he was going to take a piece out of my leg. That child had a bad upbringing, and I said, 'You're going to have to learn new manners, boy; with a stick if need be, though I'd sooner do it with philosophical dissertation and moral observations. But for now,' I continued, 'I'll say only this; that they who think country life's all maypoles and junket should come for one short visit to Roehampton.'

I set about arranging myself; looking to my pistols first, laid out on top of the tallboy, to be sure they hadn't been tampered with, and then taking off my coat and laying it nicely across a chair; for it was of a very curious cut and a tidy piece of cloth, which partly accounts for my good relations with the gentry. Then boots and britches and one thing or another and finally into my nightshirt, the little rogue watching as if he'd never seen a gentleman about his devotions before. So I was just in bed, good goosefeathers by the feel of it but very likely a harbourage for fleas, when there was a sort of scratching and rattling at the door, and I called out somewhat testily, 'For God's sake, can't a man rest? What is it now?'

It opened, and what should appear but the wench who'd eyed me with such interest in the parlour, now carrying a candle and wearing no more than a shift and a chamber robe. I was never so taken aback in my life, and demanded, 'Who in damnation are you?' to which she did a little bob and said, 'Please, sir, I'm Bet; come to see whether the bed's well aired.'

'And willing to air it for me if it ain't?' I asked.

'Yes, please, your honour,' she answered, 'if you fancy it.'

At this Maggsy, the little rogue, set up an indecent snickering, saying, 'Begod, here's a fine cock fight about to start,' and I roared at him, 'Have done, you little limb. Get out, or I'll have those clothes off your back and the skin with 'em. You shall sleep outside for that.'

'God's truth,' he whined, 'the draughts'll be the death of me; I seen it all before, master, I seen more'n . . .' But at this I leaned out to fling one of my boots at him, catching him a most gratifying clip, and he dodged behind the wench to vanish incontinently while I bawled, 'And shut the damned door after you.' Then I was more at leisure to observe the girl and I said, 'Come closer, my dear, and let's see if you'll suit.'

Well, I have seen piteous little drabs in London hawking their wares when they should have been playing with their dolls, but this one fetched me up with my mouth agape. Little more than a child herself, though of a ripe figure and a good pair of tits under her shift, the candle was shaking in her hand and for all the smile on her lips she looked as if she was clenching her teeth on a pistol ball. I will confess that I am a fair to moderate lecher when in the mood, but this offended me and I asked, 'For God's sake, how old are you, child?'

With a most sad and desperate affectation of boldness she answered, 'Plenty old enough. I'm near enough seventeen.'

'And never seen anything stiffer than a cow's udder

in your life,' I said. She blushed so bright you could perceive it running down beneath her shift, and I lost my patience, demanding, 'What sort of an old ram d'you take me for? Be off with you.'

A silly bitch nerving herself to a rude act, she just about managed to whisper, 'I'm game for anything you like; I reckon I could pick it up pretty fast.'

'You're game to get your arse slapped. I've told you; be off.'

'Please, sir.' She was weeping now. 'Let me stop. I shall be beat if you turn me away.'

'So ho?' said I. 'And who'll beat you?'

'Mr. Backus, sir. He's a terrible man in his rage.' She nodded until her pigtails bounced up and down 'Us girls has to entertain the gentlemen; and he says I'm plenty old enough to try my luck.'

I pondered that. It was likely enough; for though the more genteel may not credit this (and I hope all are genteel here) it's a common practice in some of these inns. 'So he'll beat you?' I repeated. 'Well, when I've had my breakfast – and mark that I like a pound of steak rare done and a quart of hot ale with ginger if it's a sharp morning; it keeps the bowels open – we'll see who does the beating.'

She did another little bob. 'Yes, sir. And I'm sure you'll lick Uncle Backus with one hand tied behind your back. But you'll let me stop? Because he'll beat me first.'

'God help us,' I cried. 'Isn't there any peace in this house? All right, wench. You may sit by the fire. See you keep it up all night, it'll be perishing cold before morning; and don't fidget.'

She was all smiles on the instant, saying, 'Yes, sir, thank you; I said you was a kind gentleman,' and scuttled round like a silly rabbit. For my own part I snuffed the candle and turned over, not without a chuckle at my own over niceness, but to tell the truth by no means sorry. What with one thing and another, the long journey, His Majesty's venison pie, and the better of four pints of mulled claret I was in no proper mood for further exercise and goose-feather rollicking. I was just about composing a moral observation on the situation when I dropped off to sleep; what it was I have no clear recollection, but you may be sure that it was most profound and philosophical.

For all that I was not destined to pass a quiet night. It seemed scarcely another minute before there was a squeaking and skittering, that damned hussy whispering, 'Leave go, you little wretch,' and Maggsy himself cursing in language I never thought to hear from one so tender. Not to be outdone in that direction and speaking my mind I sat up; and never shall I forget the scene. The trollop was fighting the little villain off, he clinging to her middle, with his head hard against her belly in a most unclerkly manner; he'd got the shift half off her back while she was kneeing up at him, one hand in his mop of hair, the other striking down. I roared, 'So what I don't fancy you'll take a nibble at? Well, you hot little whelp you'll need a lift to reach up to that bitch; and I'll give it you with a toe in your breech.'

They broke apart then, the hussy looking at me over her shoulder, the randy codkin peering at me from round her. 'A toe up me breech,' he squeaked. 'God's Tripes, you old fool, you was sleeping like the dead and she was going through your pockets.'

Then before you could spit she cast the boy away from her, reached out and got one of my pistols;

scarcely six feet away, gripping it in both hands, but holding it near enough at my head. I'd have sooner faced a dozen honest cut throats than that one wild bitch, weeping and desperate. I thought my last moment had come with never a breath to offer a prayer to my Maker; yet nevertheless I spoke calmly, 'Put that down; you'll do a mischief with it.'

'You'll not take my Tom,' she answered.

She had her thumbs on the flint, trying to cock it, but by good fortune she'd got the one that you have to know how to lift, though always the surest to fire, and I said, 'Who's talking of taking anybody?'

'You are,' she wept. 'You'm a thief taker. Forty pounds for a man's neck.'

'There's one thing sure,' I told her, sitting careful and still, 'you'll swing for it. You're a handsome wench to see jumping on the end of a rope. Moreover, that pistol's got a wicked backfire and you'll singe your tits. If you live long enough to pup, my girl, your brat'll screech that the milk tastes of gunpowder.'

That wavered her. She dropped her eyes and loosed one hand to pull up her shift, and at the same time she let out a squeak and smacked at the boy again; I fancy the clever little rascal had taken a nip at her backside, there being a fair round piece of it to nip at. It was all over then. I fell on her fast, twisted her arm away, took the pistol out of her grasp and fetched her a most pertinent slap myself to teach her manners. I can't put up with forward young women.

So we got her back into the chair, Maggsy grinning like a jackanapes at her dishevelment, and I said, 'Now, what was you after? Money? That'll be transportation for a start.' She shook her head and I raised my hand again. 'What then? I'll have the truth, if I have to beat it out of you. And cover yourself up, you shameless hussy.'

She turned a smoky look on the boy, snickering there, and I gave him a smack across the head to put a stop to that. Then she whispered, 'A bit of paper. Against Tom Godsave.'

'A bit of paper? What d'you mean? A warrant? Why, you silly bitch, you don't fancy we carry such things about with us, do you? Who put you up to this? Backus? Or Sir Tobias?'

'Neither. I reckoned it myself. First go off I reckoned you'd be dead drunk, and I could come in easy and look. But when you picked up with this little toad I see it couldn't be done that way. So I thought to try my luck. I thought you'd be too far gone to do anything at me. And so you was.' She near enough had the impudence to giggle.

'I've a good mind to let you see how far gone I am,' I said. 'What did you think to gain?' She did not answer and in my opinion she did not know. 'Just a thought to strike a blow for Tom Godsave?' It's a matter of amazement and wonder to me, the brave addle-witted things a woman will do when pushed to it.

'Everybody knows what thief takers are,' she muttered. 'Get their hands on some poor soul and he's as good as swinging. But you won't have my Tom.'

You must note the awful fact that there's a strong public feeling against thief takers; people cannot see that it's in their interest to help the law instead of hindering it. It's true enough that men have been hanged for the blood money before now and many thief takers, so called, have been no less rogues than the villains they set out to catch – like Mr. Jonathan Wild, and McDaniel, Salmon and Blee in '54; but it is my

32

firm belief that the most part of us these days are middling honest men, and for my part I am particular honest. In my view, moreover, it is more important to put down the present prevalence of crime and murder than it is to be overnice about how we do it, so I said, 'You've an impudent mouth, girl; you can count yourself lucky I don't slap it for you to teach you manners. If your Tom stole my Lady Hartingfield's jewels he'll hang. If he didn't he'll go free. And that I shall see to myself.'

'He didn't,' she said. 'He couldn't have.'

'And why not, pray?' I asked.

'He's bashful. Tom's afraid of nothing in trousers but overnice with women. In particular Lady Louise-Marie.' A smell of jealousy there, I noted; and for the first time the little termagant had stopped being frightened. 'Tom could no more've threatened her with a pistol in his hand than pigs might fly.'

'So,' I mused, considering the wench, 'if bashful Tom didn't filch my lady's jewels, who could it be? Sir Tobias? Or Captain Roderick Medfield?'

'Sir Toby's naught to do with us,' she answered, a shade too fast, I thought. 'But Captain Roderick's a rare wicked roaring man.'

'So,' I said again, 'if Captain Roderick's the highwayman, where's Thomas Godsave?'

She shook her head. 'I don't know. Nobody's seen hide nor hair of him these two days past.'

It was sticking out like a parson's nose that if she was sweet about the man she was uncommonly at ease not knowing where he was, and I lifted my hand to her again saying, 'Listen, girl. I want answers and I'm not overnice how I get 'em. Where is he?'

'I've told you fair and square. I don't know.'

33

Though sorely tempted I changed my mind about striking her; for there are some women better treated soft, so they think they can take advantage, to their own fatal undoing. 'Very well then, I've done with you. Mend the fire and be off.'

'You mean to go?'

'What else? Be damned, I've had enough of you this night; or any other in a lifetime for that matter.' She stared at me and then turned to the fire, raking it up and sweeping the hearth, putting fresh logs on, while I watched the boy considering her rump, thinking lascivious thoughts no doubt as they are apt to do at that age. Then I asked. 'What sort of people are out upon the heath, there?'

'Oh the wickedest,' she answered blithely, 'they'd cut your liver out for tuppence. A band of tinkers over by the windmill and a camp of gipsy horse dealers in the woods, to say nothing of runaway sailors lying up at the Green Man, and the drovers at the inn by the telegraph. And a charcoal burner who's said to turn his hand to anything.'

'A right nest of rogues,' I observed. 'Seems to me this Roehampton's somewhat worse than Sodom and Gomorrah. Depend upon it that's where your Tom is, with that last-named rascal, for there's nothing like a charcoal heap for ridding yourself of a body; it cooks quiet and slow. He'll be done to a turn by now,' I told her comfortably, getting myself back into bed. 'You'll never make much use of what he's got between his legs, my girl.' She was bold enough to giggle at that, the naughty bitch, thus proving that she knew better, but I let her have it; there was time enough to deal with Mistress Bet at my leisure, and I finished, 'I'll sleep on it whether to give you over to the constable tomorrow;

if I do that'll be transportation at least. Mind I get that pound of steak for my breakfast. If it comes the way I like it, I might be sweeter tempered afterwards, but I wouldn't swear to it.'

'You'm a wicked monster, and you should watch lest somebody don't cut your own throat for you,' she cried, and ran from the room.

'As for you,' I asked the boy when she'd gone, 'how did you come to know what she was about?'

'Peeking through the keyhole,' he answered unabashed. 'I reckoned I might see a good bit of sport. Likewise it was wicked cold out there; I thought when you'd done her to your liking and gone to sleep I could creep back in and get against the fire.'

'Peeking through the keyhole,' I said, 'shows a proper sense of the art and mystery of detection. So it's a nice matter whether to knock you sideways or commend you for it. You shall perceive a moral observation here; that often what you start for ill will turn out good, and contrariwise what you begin with fondest hopes'll sometimes do a deal of harm. Only the Lord knows, and He never lets on; though Jeremy Sturrock generally contrives to find out.'

'I was of two minds to let her shoot you,' he confessed. 'But I thought of my new clothes and regular tucker for a week or two, until you tire of me. Only I never seen a man shot. I seen a watchman once get his tripes cut out, but I never seen a man shot.'

'You'll see a common little rogue hung up by his heels to roast in a minute,' I threatened, though too comfortable to attend to it at that moment. 'But for now let's have some quiet. We've clever work to do tomorrow, and as pretty a little mystery as ever I've seen to solve. In short, I fancy it, Master Maggsy.' So I addressed me again to sleep as Mr. William Shakespeare puts it; I take great pleasure in going to the play and when in polite company frequently recount my recollections of the incomparable Mrs. Siddons as Lady Macbeth, although some years back now.

The rest of the night was peaceful and I awoke with no more than a light touch of the livers. The boy was snoring on the hearth and I prodded him up to attend me at my toilet, about which I am very nice even in outlandish places, made him wash himself after me especially behind the ears, and then we descended; not without several improving observations on my part. There was a gaggle of cleaning wenches about, but no sign of Mistress Bet, and the fire was already ablaze in the parlour, where I took my pound of steak with side trimmings and a quart of ale. The same for the boy, but somewhat less on account of his smaller stature, instructing him in genteel table behaviour the while, in particular not to slobber the grease all over his chaps.

We'd just about done when Mr. Backus came in, all geniality, though looking with some ill-favour at Maggsy, plainly not liking to see him so promoted. But he said nothing of it, only asking, 'Did you have a good night, Mr. Sturrock; and is all to your liking?'

'Very fair,' I answered, 'and a tidy cut of steak,' mopping up the gravy off my plate with a hunk of bread and taking a last draught of ale; at the same time reflecting about that wild and desperate wench daring her belly and her fortune for the sake of poor Tom Godsave, and wondering how much this fellow knew about the happenings last night. To put him to the test I said, 'And a very fair bed. I'd have thought you might've found me some warm company, though.

It's the custom of many places.'

'Not this one. I'm not over delicate, you'll understand; I like a rattle well enough myself now and again. But I leave whore shops to them as knows best how to run 'em.'

Maggsy looked as if he was about to pipe up with some untoward outrageousness and I gave him a sharp hard kick under the table for there was no need to split on Mistress Bet at this moment; there might be a time for that later on, if I considered it worth while. 'You're very wise,' I answered. 'Is my post boy about?'

'Around the stables. There's word that Putney Hill's blocked beyond the Green Man, and he declares he can't get through to London and won't try.'

'More like he fancies your good provender and ale better; and no doubt chalking it up to my account, the rogue. So he might as well make himself useful. Have him put the horses in and be ready to take me to Hartingfield.'

'You'll wait upon my lord, then?'

'It's what I'm here for. We must have this business settled.' I resolved on a sudden, sharp question. 'It's certain sure that Sir Tobias was waiting here for me yesterday. So what's his interest in Thomas Godsave?'

He gave me one of his sidelong looks before answering. 'Like all the rest of us Sir Toby don't think Tom did it. I'd fancy he's a mind to keep close by you, Mr. Sturrock, in case the lad needs some help when you do find him.'

I thought of Sir Tobias last night saying that the rogue'd be well away to London by now, but said, 'A very proper sentiment for a local gentleman. He'll be well liked about here?'

'He's a good friend and a good master.'

'And a well known gambler and sportsman, so I'm told. Tell me, Mr. Backus, as between the pair of us, has it come to your notice that he's been losing any very considerable sums of money lately?'

'Sir Toby?' Backus stared, and then looked as if he was going to laugh at me. 'You're on the wrong tack, Mr. Sturrock. He's one of the wealthiest men in the county. And I've never seen a better judge of a horse; nor of a fighting cock nor a pugilist come to that.'

As he was saying this the girl Bet appeared at the door, crying, 'Uncle Backus, you'm wanted,' but plainly hotfoot to see what I was telling him about her, and not without a glance of apprehension at me. But I gave her a benevolent look and said, 'Why, you're a pretty creature, my dear; and if my breakfast was your handiwork a gentle soul with a pound of steak into the bargain.'

She did a bob in exchange, turning pink, though still with a sparkle of mischief in her eyes, the little besom. 'Thank you, sir; you'm very kind, I'm sure.'

'My niece Bet,' Backus explained, with some pride. 'Her father's like me, a widower; and at present a bo'sun with Admiral Nelson. Was at the engagement of Cape St. Vincent, and Aboukir Bay; as we had news only last week.'

'Why then,' I announced, 'we must make occasion to drink his health; we owe these gallant fellows more than we dream of yet. And we'll see to it that Mistress Bet shall take a little glass of something with us.' Leaving the chit still wondering, I added, 'But we must be about our business. Yet first one more matter, Mr. Backus; and an easier one this time. You'll not credit it, but I've a memory like a sieve. Before I travelled out here an old friend of mine, a sea captain, said I was to be sure and call on some relation of his. A female and a merry soul, but a rare gossip.' This you shall note was a piece of cunning, for there is always one such wherever you go and a fine specimen is often of a value above rubies in the art and science of detection. 'But, damn me,' I finished with a laugh, 'I've forgotten the creature's name.'

'A rare gossip,' Backus said, snorting down his nose. 'Then for certain you'll be meaning the Widow Quince. You'll never find a rarer. That one's tongue's hitched in the middle and wags both ends. She's at Dover Cottage, across Roehampton Lane.'

'That's it,' I cried, 'that's the name; Quince. I'm obliged to you, Mr. Backus.' With that I lifted the lad from the table by his ear, not before he'd cleared pretty well everything there was on it, and we set to muffling ourselves up against the cold.

The snow was holding off, but it was a lowering sky, and that pestilential heath was all dark trees and thickets, the better of a woodsman's axe to the greater part of it. Our post boy was still as surly as ever, very likely at being dragged away from his rude and bawdy talk with the ostlers, but young Maggsy was all agog at taking a ride like a lord; I don't suppose the rascal had ever enjoyed such a full belly before, and I hoped he was properly grateful for it. He asked, 'Are we agoing to catch somebody to hang?'

With my liver nicely settled and in the mood for disquisition I answered, 'We are about the first part of detection, which consists of gathering all of the information not only pertaining to, but also surrounding the said act of felony, to the end of discovering which rogues are lying and which honest people, if any, are telling the truth.'

He said, 'I see a hanging once, Three of 'em at one go; I didn't reckon much of it. Nothing to the job except a drop and a jerk.'

'You are a most horrible child,' I told him, 'and I shall surely consider casting you off again if you don't improve yourself. A public hanging is a salutary spectacle, not a raree show. It ought properly to be an occasion of sorrow and moral observation.'

The little monster went on, 'As to moral observation there was plenty and enough of that. One of 'em said, "Good people all I freely confess my black and wicked crimes as I hope for mercy from my dread Maker when I meet Him face to face any minute now, and I beg all you good people who witness me here in this solemn and awful predicament to pray for my soul as you wish for salvation to your own".' He took a breath and finished up, 'God's truth, in his place I'd have cried out "Sod the lot of you and I wisht you was all up here with a rope round your necks like I am now".'

The only answer to such wicked blasphemy was a sharp correction, but my philosophical mood was spoiled and, moreover, on that instant the post boy drew up the horses. He was bending over talking to a lumpish yokel standing with the snow above his calves and I leaned out to ask, 'For God's sake, what's the matter now?'

'This chap wants to know if we's the surgeon,' he snarled back at me. 'Says there's somethin' amiss at the Hall.'

'Then for God's sake,' I bawled at him, 'let's get there this side of doomsday and discover what it is.'

We turned off down a little lane, lurching in the ruts beneath the snow and winding between one farmhouse and another and here and there a labourer's cot-

40

tage, until we came to a pair of gate posts and an empty lodge. A mean place with the gates rusted on their hinges; on the drive two sets of hoof marks looking as if the animals had been ridden hard by the way the snow was scattered, and ahead of us the Hall itself – near enough as lapsed in decay as the lodge and what my master's old clerk, with his Gothick fancy, would doubtless describe as a gloomy pile.

When we got to the steps the front doors were agape and I jangled on the bell pull and went in. It was certain Lord Hartingfield was a skinflint for there were no fires lit, even at this hour, and the place was as cold as the tomb, though it was a fair enough hall had some attention ever been paid to it. Nor was there a soul to be seen, but somewhere within there was a chattering and wailing of women, so I rapped my cane upon the pavement and cried, 'Hulloa, there!'

After a time there came a slow shuffling from under the staircase and a stringy, whey-faced fellow appeared, wearing a drab snuff-coloured livery and an old-fashioned wig that hadn't seen the smell of powder in a month of Sundays. A footman; but a footman of the most doltish and inferior kind, and he asked. 'Who be you?'

'That's for your betters,' I told him. 'I'm here to wait upon your master.'

'Begod,' he answered uncivilly, 'you'll wait till the devil turns into a duck then, for my lord's as dead as a louse. Throttled and killed this very last night. And my lady sitting up in her chamber and laughing her head off.'

It is not my custom to be taken aback, yet even I was silenced, as much by the fellow's insolence as his news.

But I raised my cane to him, saying. 'Then it seems I'm most needed here. The Bow Street Runners, my man. And you may take me this instant to whoever's left in charge.'

III

The fellow still hung back and while I was debating whether to lay my cane about his shoulders another approached from a doorway to the side of the hall; plainly of a better sort than the first, yet still like nothing so much as an old sheep dressed in black, and frightened. An elderly fiftyish I should judge and, apart from a flush of port about his nose, a pale and miserable figure of a man. He asked, 'What is this, Hack?' and the other answered, 'Her says from Bow Street Runners, Mr. Gotobed.'

'And needed here by the look of it,' I broke in. 'What's this the fellow tells me?' But while the older one was gathering his wits to speak a woman came out to stand beside him, likewise dressed in black, and a thin beanpole with a face as pale as the other and eyes like black smudges, but plain enough the authority in this house. I addressed myself to her. 'Mr. Sturrock, ma'am. Officer of the Bow Street Runners. His lordship wrote for us the day before yesterday; but now it seems that there's more amiss than the matter of my lady's diamonds. And if I may be so bold?'

'I am Mrs. Gotobed, housekeeper to his lordship; and Mr. Gotobed is our butler. Hack,' she snapped at the other fellow, 'be about your business,' and he turned away with a surly stare while she gave her poor husband a hard look and then announced to me, 'His late lordship. Not two hours since my lord was found done to death and murdered.' She might have been saying the linen had been misfolded.

'Then why do we stand here?' I asked; but with my remarkable quick mind thinking of Maggsy and of a good use for him. I said, 'This here is my clerk. Have him taken to the kitchen where he can await me. And you, boy,' I told him, 'remember your place. Say nothing, but listen when you're spoke to. D'you understand?' I knew then that my instinct of last night had not been wrong and the little rascal would earn his keep; for he gave me a sharp look and nodded and said, 'Yes, master; I understand.'

Gotobed bowed, but still seemed to ask permission of the woman, which she answered by nodding briefly, before he led the boy away. At the same time madam regarded me with no particular favour and with some impatience I repeated, 'Bow Street, ma'am; and by the look of it the properest person to be here.' Then she answered, 'Be good enough to follow me,' and led the way to a door on the left-hand side of the hall into a sort of business room or cabinet.

I shall describe this for you with care. It was somewhat dark on account of the panelling, and as cold as the grave. It had a double window in the French fashion, of which a single pane of glass near the handle on one side was broke, with the curtains half drawn back; and on this same side a patch of wet on the floor and still some trace of melted snow. The ashes of a dead fire on the hearth, never at any time a very big one; a writing table or desk, and on this a few papers, a candelabra with the candles in it half burned down but not guttered all that much, and a tray holding quills and a stick or two of red wax. Besides this we had a high-backed chair thrown sideways on the carpet – on that side of the desk which whoever was sitting

44

there would have been facing the window – another quill near enough snapped in half and, lying with the blade open under the chair itself, a common horn-handled knife such as grooms or ostlers carry. And, not least, the figure shrouded with a sheet and lying most ungainly on a sofa.

For a while I considered all this, fixing it upon the inner eye as it were, before lifting back the cover to look down on the mortal remains of my Lord Harting-field; a man of approaching sixty, I judged, and of a somewhat frail figure. Even in life he could scarcely have been a lovesome object; in this manner of death I have rarely seen worse cut down from the drop at Newgate, for they at least hang straight. As my inten-tion here is a mere diverting tale I shall not describe the face, the swollen tongue, blue flesh and staring eyes; but he was frozen hard in the attitude as he must have lain all night, like a poor rag doll thrown aside and forgotten. Even for a skinflint it was a bad death.

Him I considered too, studying his position and the brutal evidence about his throat and, even more closely, a sort of crescent-shaped bruise or contusion – not much darkened yet – on the right side of the fore-head. Then I looked at the hands. They were clean enough except that the thumb and first two fingers of the right were stained with ink and, driven hard under the nail of that thumb, was a fragment of some substance which puzzled me until on examining it closer I perceived to be wax; but not like that on the desk, this being a brownish colour. Apart from these indications there seemed little more to be had from my lord and at length I drew back the cover.

With the woman watching me still I gave my atten-tion next to the window. Here I found only one piece of glass lying within the room and so far as I could see no more outside; but the snow was drifted there to perhaps a foot or more. I murmured, 'So ho,' as I do when finding food for thought, and went back to the desk. On this, as I have said, there were several sheets of paper; but, you will note, none with any writing on it. Reflecting on this too I turned to the fire grate; yet there was no sign of paper ash here, the remains of the logs alone lying as they had at length burned out, and undisturbed. Finally I took up the broken quill and the knife and examined these before laying them aside; the first had been newly sharpened but used afterwards, and the other having a rough letter 'T' scratched or filed into the handle.

'Well now,' I said to the woman, who was standing there as quiet as the corpse itself and not a lot prettier, 'here we've a teasing business. Who discovered him? And when?'

'The footman,' she answered. 'Hack. About eight o'clock when he came in here to clean the hearth and make the fire.'

'And at what hour last night would the fire be made up?'

'Not after nine. His lordship was careful.' I looked through the window at the dark forest of the heath, not a mile away, and she smiled a little bit. 'It was more a matter of the candles than wood; they are not to be had for the asking.'

'A very proper spirit,' I observed. 'Was the window open when Hack came in this morning?'

'Yes. I had it closed. And the snow swept up.'

I nodded, for that was reasonable. 'So my lord was discovered two hours since. What have you done?'

'What must needs be. My lady was informed.'

'My lady was informed,' I repeated, reflecting that from this it would appear they slept apart; perhaps not surprising for his lordship clearly had been no ardent young lover. 'I must talk to my lady before long,' I continued, 'when we've finished here. What else did you do?'

'We despatched a groom to the physician, Doctor Nokes, in Putney; he is also the coroner. But it may be late before he arrives. He is known to sit over his port at night and they say the snow is thick on the Hill. And we sent for Sir Tobias Westleigh.'

'Sir Tobias Westleigh? Was he a friend then of my lord?'

Once more she came as near to smiling as she could. 'He is Justice of the Peace. And the Parish Constable is useless.'

Standing at the window I reflected that Sir Tobias was a damned odd Justice too, but maybe no odder than many others in these wild country places. Even as she spoke I saw two horsemen approaching at a hard gallop up the drive; Sir Tobias himself with a groom following. He flung himself off his animal at the steps with cloak flying and tossed the reins to his man; we heard him tramping in the hall and the voice of Gotobed, and then he appeared in the doorway saying, 'Damnation, he might've picked a better day for it,' stopping and turning his hard look on me. 'Good day to you, sir,' he said, 'it seems you're hot upon the mischief,' and marched across to the couch to draw back the sheet and stand gazing down at my lord with a look which I could not read, though I had my guesses; the chief being that there was no love lost between them. 'Yes,' he observed, 'for certain that's a matter for the coroner. By God, he makes an ugly corpse,' and added

47

to me, 'well, sir, there's villainy enough here to suit you.'

'Very near,' I agreed. 'And maybe more than we know of.'

'What d'you mean by that?' he demanded.

'All in good time, sir,' I promised. 'In the meanwhile we'll have the footman Hack in.'

It did not escape my notice that Gotobed looked to his wife and waited until she nodded before he went to fetch the fellow, while Sir Tobias remarked, 'No doubt you'll be putting your art and mystery of detection to work, Mr. Sturrock.'

'After my own fashion,' I answered, 'and you may be sure it will lead us to our man.'

I was somewhat brisk with him, and he gave one of his short laughs. 'I ask your pardon, Mr. Sturrock. I'm a little out of humour this morning. Our Backus's mulled claret is a confounded liverish liquor, don't you find? What of her ladyship?' he asked the woman.

She paused for long enough to notice, but then answered, 'Deeply shocked, sir. She begs to remain in her parlour.'

'We'll let the lady rest,' I told them, soft but certain. 'For the time we've work to do here.' Gotobed came back on this, bringing the footman before him, and I said sharply, 'Come, Hack, we'll have straight answers to simple questions. When you entered here this morning what did you see?'

'Why, precious little,' he grunted. 'Candle nigh on blew out in the draught from the window, and I near enough tripped over'n. His lordship.'

'And what did you do then?'

'Set down my brush and pan and hollered. What d'you expect?'

'Keep a civil tongue, my man,' I warned him.

'Hack shouted, sir,' Gotobed said, 'and I came from my pantry. Then we both saw that his lordship was stiff and cold, and I called Mrs. Gotobed.'

I looked at the woman and she continued, 'I told Hack to light the other candles. Then it was certain at once that there was nothing to be done and I had Mr. Gotobed and Hack lift him on to the sofa, while I closed the window. It did not seem proper to leave him lying there.'

'The window was open, and a draught near enough to gutter Hack's candle out,' I observed. 'Yet my lord's paper is all laid there on the desk. Didn't that blow about then?'

There was a sharp silence at this until Mrs. Gotobed answered, 'If I am at fault I ask pardon. But I gathered it all and replaced it.'

'And why not?' I asked warmly. 'Very proper, ma'am; for tidiness is a virtue. But tell me this; was there any with writing on?'

'No, sir,' Mrs. Gotobed replied sharply, 'there was not.'

Since I had already observed this for myself I was not all that surprised, but Sir Tobias burst out, 'Is there any matter in all this?'

'As to that, sir,' I told him, 'it's what we have to find out. Now,' I finished, 'this knife. Whose is it? Does any of you know?'

'It's such as the stable men use,' Gotobed volunteered.

'That for certain,' Hack said, 'for 'tis Tom Godsave's. If you look you'll see a figure "T" cut on it. He done that easy, but couldn't compass the next one, that being roundy like and harder.'

'Tom Godsave's,' I mused, looking at Sir Tobias who was plainly nonplussed. 'It was found under the chair here, sir. Poor Thomas Godsave. You'll be prepared to swear to that, Hack?' I asked.

'I don't aim to swear to nothing,' he muttered.

'You might have to yet,' I told him. 'Now; the fire was made up at nine o'clock last night. By you?' He nodded, and I continued, 'And my lord was alive then or you'd have noticed for sure. What was he doing?'

'Asharpening a quill. And in a proper wicked temper. He cussed me roundly and told me to have done and get out.'

'Sharpening a quill,' I repeated. 'With this blade?'

'Certainly not,' Mrs. Gotobed snapped. 'My lord always used a silver pen knife.'

'I'm obliged to you, ma'am,' I said. 'And you may go now, Hack; unless Sir Tobias has any questions to ask.'

'God's faith,' answered Sir Tobias, 'you're asking enough, sir.'

'As befits my duty. And there's more yet. Mr. Gotobed; it will be your business to go round last thing and see to all the doors, windows and lights.' He bowed, which I took to mean that it was, and I asked, 'Did you come in here? And at what hour?'

'The doors were all fast, sir. And I did come in here. At a little after ten. I asked my lord's pardon and went to look to this window. That was fastened also. Then I enquired whether he required anything further and he told me I could retire.'

'His lordship would very likely be writing at the desk by then. Did you happen to see what it was?'

The man gawped at me. 'It would not be my place, sir.'

'Very proper,' I commended him. 'Yet a pity since it leaves us with something we do not know. But we must make shift without it. You came in after ten and the fire was mended at nine. What was it like then?'

'It was burning through, sir. I asked his lordship if I should make it but he told me to let it be.'

Considering now whether to ask had anything been stolen or purloined, deciding that it would be a wasted question since I already knew the answer, I turned then to Mrs. Gotobed. 'I will now wait upon my Lady Hartingfield.'

'By God, sir,' Sir Tobias barked on the instant, 'you'll do no such thing; not in this state of affairs,' and Mrs. Gotobed herself answered, 'Her ladyship is indisposed.'

'Not half an hour since,' I said, 'that surly fellow of yours claimed she was laughing her head off. It's a strange indisposition.'

'On the contrary,' madam observed, 'it's a very common one. She was laughing and weeping and babbling all together.'

'She'll be recovered by now.' Sir Tobias slapped his riding crop against his boots and looked likely to burst out again, but I continued, 'Sir Tobias, there's been a robbery of above thirty thousand and a most damnable murder on top of it. And I'll remind you that the law brooks no interference. You as a Justice should commend that.' Turning again to the woman, I finished, 'Be so good as to present my respects to her ladyship. Tell her that I would not wish to intrude upon her grief. Yet I shall wait on her directly; at her convenience, but not too long.'

Seeming about to start wringing his hands Gotobed left the room and the woman followed him with another sour look at me, while Sir Tobias fetched the desk a hard crack with his whip saying, 'You take too much on yourself. But I'll come up with you.'

'No, sir,' I answered softly. 'I want to see my lady alone.'

'Then want'll be your master,' he roared. 'I'll come with you.'

In a voice even softer I said, 'Sir, if you persist in this I shall conclude there is something you do not wish my lady to tell me.' He was a young man, and sound and spare, but for a minute I thought he was about to have an apoplexy; or what was worse to slash me with his crop, in which case I should have been forced to defend myself by laying violent hands upon the gentry. Nevertheless I continued, 'Sir Tobias, I'm your servant as befits my position; but I'll see to my own work or go back to London. And if I do Tom Godsave will hang for certain. For every particle of evidence we have here points to him.' I did not say that every particle likewise was false evidence, keeping that dark for my own reasons, but continued, 'And depend upon it he'll be found wherever he's hiding, since a Peer of the Realm is not to be murdered lightly.'

That steadied him, though his face was still dark, and he observed, 'God's Teeth, my man, you're a hardy rogue.'

'I need to be, sir,' I rejoined, 'I deal with hardy people.'

Recovering himself, he had the grace to laugh at that saying, 'Very well, if you must; but see you mind your manners,' and the woman Gotobed returned then from announcing me to my lady. She said, 'Her ladyship will receive you now,' and added for Sir

Tobias, 'She begs also that you will wait upon her afterwards sir.'

We went out and up the great stairs, well polished and fine enough if your taste lies in the old-fashioned style, with a few darkish pictures, of which I confess to no judgement having little knowledge of such things although I know what takes my fancy. Then along a decent corridor, except the carpet was somewhat worn, and at last to a door upon which Mrs. Gotobed scratched and stood aside to let me in. A bright, pretty little chamber with furniture after the frippish French style, female flounces and elegances and, thank God, a good fire burning on the hearth; I was near enough frozen myself by then.

Attired in a blue mantle trimmed with white fur my lady was reclining on a day bed with a dish of chocolate beside her. She did not rise or hold out her hand, considering me from a pair of cool, greyish-hazel eyes; dark hair with ringlets, not yet dressed but piled up atop of her head, an oval face not pale nor yet too over-coloured, and a full mouth. You could say beautiful if you liked that manner, and perhaps sufficiently soft in the right company; but to my mind marred by an over-firm chin which in a few years might well become the battle prow of a shrew. Nevertheless you could see in her the true aristocracy to which we must all pay our respects, even though it be French, and I advanced my knee in my best bow, saying, 'My lady, pray let me offer my most sincere sympathy and condolence for this grievous business. Jeremy Sturrock of the Bow Street Runners, and your servant.'

Speaking in as good English as my own, even a little better for I am a blunt spoken man, but touched with a certain preciseness and sibilance, she answered, 'Mr.

Sturrock, for the manner of my husband's death one must grieve, as any decent person should. For the fact of it, I shall attend his funeral with some equanimity.'

That, as my old sea captain friend would have said, fetched me up all standing. But I answered, 'It is to the manner of his lordship's end that there are certain questions, my lady.'

'And I shall answer them if I can,' she promised.

If you consider fit, I thought, noting also that she did not ask me to be seated. 'At the time his lordship was attacked it appears that he was writing. A letter perhaps; a memorandum of estate business; perhaps his personal diary. Yet nothing of this can now be found. Do you know what such writing might have been?'

To a less keen eye than mine it might have passed as fancy; but I marked a certain hesitation before she answered, 'I do not. Hartingfield had his own affairs in which I never meddled. Do you say this writing, whatever it was, might have had some part in his death?'

'That is a chance which must be considered. As we must consider whether your jewels and Thomas Godsave had a part in it.'

She lowered her eyelids, gazing at me from under long, dark lashes. 'Ah yes; my jewels.'

'They are worth about thirty thousand, as I understand.'

'Considerably above.'

'Presented to you doubtless by his lordship?'

Her eyes opened wide at me again; compounded of astonishment and mockery. 'You are somewhat impudent,' she said. 'And with a strange idea of his lordship. Hartingfield would not give the devil a coal for hell fire except in the hope to warm himself by it and save the kindling. The jewels were my own property, or the property of my family. My mother, the marquise, and I brought them with us when we escaped France in '92.'

I bowed again, saying, 'I stand properly corrected.'

She continued, 'I do not need to tell you this, but I shall because I choose to have these things clearly understood. We came from France leaving my father and elder brother; who had a devotion to their majesties and could not see it in their duty to escape. They were disgustingly butchered in the Terror; whereon my mother died of shock and despondency. I was left in need of protection; there were rumours that London was full of revolutionary agents seeking out émigrés who had escaped with valuables. How true that was I still do not know, but it seemed likely enough then. And Hartingfield . . .' She checked for an instant and then added, 'Hartingfield offered the shelter and security of an English title.' She stopped suddenly again before bursting out, 'And I now say damnation to all politics; and in particular God's damnation to these swine who preach brotherhood and practise slaughter.' Yet once more this surprising creature stopped; and at last finished lightly, 'Lord, sir, I carry myself away.'

'You carry me with you,' I said. 'I most heartily agree and approve; for we've all too many of these crackpot Whigs and canting dissenters in this country, and we shall have trouble with them before we've done. My deepest sympathy, ma'am; and I'm honoured by your confidence.' But business must go on, and I asked, 'Yet may we now come to the matter of the robbery and felony itself?'

'Willingly,' she answered.

'As I understand you were returning from Portsmouth.'

'From Alton, to be precise. From my Lady Sayle's where I had been visiting three days for a coming-of-age ball. Hartingfield had no stomach for such affairs; but I was determined on it, and he could not prevent me taking my jewels.'

'You were travelling without attendants?'

'My Lady Sayle sent an armed groom with us, as far as Kingston; but the fellow's horse cast a shoe at some village ten miles before that and there was nothing for him to do but to look for a smithy. It was already showing sign of early dark and I insisted we drive on without him. Our own groom was to have waited on us at Kingston, but when we came there neither had he arrived; again I ordered the coachman to go forward.'

'And the groom who was to have met you there?'

Again I detected a small pause; 'Thomas Godsave.'

'Once more Thomas Godsave,' I observed. 'The fellow haunts this affair like Hamlet's father. So you drove on. Were the coach lamps lit?'

'My coachman, Buckle, lit them at Gallows Hill. The horses were tired and I near enough half asleep myself; I remember no more until I heard this voice crying something and Buckle reined in so sharp I was near thrown off my seat. Upon that, in a fine temper, I thrust my head from the window and demanded what the matter was and Buckle answered, "A highwayman, my lady." A moment later the fellow appeared and said "Your jewel box, milady, and be smart about it".'

'So ho,' I said. 'And Buckle did nothing?'

'What could he do? The fellow had two pistols, one

trained upon him and the other on myself. I cursed him finely, not being light about such insolence, but he motioned with these pistols and I thrust the jewel case out. Had he shot Buckle I myself would have been at his mercy. It seemed best to be rid of him.'

'As you say, ma'am,' I observed. 'There's no arguing with a highwayman. Now Buckle swears it was Thomas Godsave. Did you yourself perceive him so clearly? When we have the rascal before a judge would you swear to him?'

'It was very dark. He was wearing a cloth or cap over his head with two holes cut out for eyes. A frightful sight in itself. Under it his voice was hoarse and muffled.'

I gazed at her, considering. 'What would you say, ma'am, if I suggested it was one, Captain Roderick Medfield?'

'Medfield?' Plainly that was a new thought to her, and she narrowed her eyes over it. 'Medfield?' she repeated. 'Why certainly he'd fit the part. He's a rogue both by nature and by inclination.'

'But could you swear to him?'

'Lord, sir,' she cried, 'it was dark as the pit in that damnation forest. The business was done in a minute. While I was in a rare terror and no state to recognise the Archangel Gabriel. It's your business to find this villain, not mine to swear.'

Bowing to her once more I answered, 'No doubt your coachman had leisure to observe the whole matter,' and adding, 'I thank you for your kindness,' turned to the door. But there I asked, 'Would it not be customary, ma'am, for a lady of your state to travel with a maid?'

'Commonly, yes,' she answered, indifferent again.

'But I am without one for the time. My last wench was becoming very pert, taking upon herself too many of these revolutionary notions. In the end I sent her packing; these several weeks since.'

'And where is she now?'

My lady raised her shoulders; a Frenchified gesture I cannot put up with. 'For all I know or care on the streets of London.'

'Ma'am,' I said, 'there's information been passed in this business. Where your coach might be best held up, and when. Is it like that she and Medfield might have worked together?'

She narrowed her eyes at me again. 'I believe you've hit upon something. It is like, sir. For she knew several months back that I was to visit my Lady Sayle. It's very like indeed.'

I bowed myself out; and I shall not yet confess to you what was in my mind, but by now no doubt you will have perceived several matters of interest for yourself. By no means dissatisfied I took my way down the stairs again.

They had lit a fire in my lord's cabinet, not before time. Sir Tobias was there and Gotobed with him, looking like wringing his hands again, and another one; by his manner and method the physician. A face as red as a cock turkey's arse and also much resembling the same in other respects, and he was roaring, 'Blast you, Gotobed, fetching me out of a day like this. Even you could see there's nothing to be done for him. He'd have kept until tomorrow.'

Sir Tobias, who seemed to have recovered his humour, was most unseemly amused. He said, 'Doctor Nokes, we have here Mr. Jeremy Sturrock. A most notable exponent and master of the art and science

58

of detection.'

'Detection?' the other bellowed. 'Fartation. You don't want no detection here, it's as plain as a pregnant drab. Death from suffocation and stoppage of the heart brought about by strangulation of the windpipe. Couldn't a been an accident, couldn't a done it himself, therefore wilful murder. Find that rascal Godsave and hang him and you've got it over with. Wish you good day. Inquest tomorrow. No, God dammit, can't do that, I'm bidden to dine with Mr. Rucker; inquest the day after, in the forenoon. Put him in the ice house to have him fresh, Gotobed.'

Now I was in a somewhat quandarious situation. For though wanting it put about that Godsave was the guilty party, thus forcing him out of hiding because he must needs declare where he was at the critical hour to save himself, I was loath to let it seem that the pitiful mess of false evidence here had taken me in. Moreover, I suffered a most inordinate desire to remove the bung from this sounding barrel of stale port. But I hit upon a happy solution. I said, 'Sir; at what hour last night would you calculate my lord met his death?'

He gazed at me with his eyes very near falling out of his head, crying, 'God's Tripes, man, how do I know, or care? What does it matter?'

At my most genteel I answered, 'If it should happen that Godsave can prove his whereabouts at that precise time we shall have no case.' Sir Tobias still had his air of unseemly humour, while the learned doctor looked like a seizure, but I continued unperturbed, 'It will be as well to inform you here, in the presence of Sir Tobias and Mr. Gotobed. My Lord Hartingfield was attacked and murdered at some time between the hours of a quarter gone ten and half after eleven last night. And if you direct your jury you'll do well to bear that fact in mind.'

Gotobed looked as if the world had come to an end, and our fine physician seemed closer to a seizure than ever. 'Begod,' he burst out, 'are you daring to instruct me? We want none of your saucy London tricks here, my man; we're sensible folk on our own dung heap and we know best how to conduct our own business. I say my verdict'll be murder against Godsave. And I'll be off, Gotobed, before this impudent upstart drives me into an apoplexy.'

He stamped off with Gotobed following; we heard him roaring down the hall and watched him a minute later, muffled in his cloaks and capes, clambering into his carriage, still cursing and brandishing his stick at the coachman. Then Sir Tobias observed, 'Well, sir, you've not endeared yourself. And you've as good as done for Godsave. Do I understand you're certain of him now?'

'The evidence points that way,' I answered. 'I've a hope that Gotobed might put it around through the servants; and the precise time of the murder. So Godsave might come out of hiding to clear himself. If he can.'

'Damn it,' he said. 'You offer the poor devil little choice. Come out and confess to highway robbery; stay hid and be hunted for murder.' He turned away from the window to glance at the still figure under its sheets on the sofa. 'Gotobed should get that out of here; by the time our worthy coroner has his jury in to view it'll give 'em convulsions. Confound this business, Sturrock; it's running out of hand. Did you have any good of my lady?'

'Not a lot,' I confessed. 'Only small matters which I

have not yet had time to consider. And it seemed to me that she was most curious indifferent.'

He looked at me sharply. 'Indifferent? Don't let that fox you; it's an affectation of hers. Get her jewels back, sir; she'll not be indifferent then.' He gave one of his sudden short laughs and added, 'I'd best go up to pay my own respects. And I'll give myself the pleasure of waiting on you at the King's Head tonight.'

'It will be my privilege, sir,' I told him. And when he had gone I went across to my lord and turned the sheet back again, considering that bruise on his forehead and the fragment of wax under the thumb nail. I said, 'Well, my lord, I'll make but one proposition. That this affair has as many bones in it as a herring; and some of them are already starting to itch in my throat.' And upon that observation I turned to the door to set about my investigation in the other parts of the house.

IV

There was nobody about in the hall, and I stood surveying it. Seeing it thus, with your back to the main porch, there was two doors to each side, these no doubt being the reception rooms; which I did not trouble to look into then. You had the great staircase directly in front going up in two wings and under this two more doors; but these barely seen, being fashioned to match the general panelling. They would be the service quarters and, now being out to find my way to the back of the house and in particular the stables, I first tried the right-hand one. As I thought, it was lined in green baize with a stone-flagged passage beyond, several more doors yet and a flight of back stairs; and also a smell of cooking and a considerable chatter of voices. This clearly was the kitchens and so on, where I hoped Master Maggsy was at present keeping his ears well open, and not wishing to interrupt – for my presence sometimes has a silencing effect on the lower sort – I turned back to the fellow door on the left.

This again was lined with baize, and a passage beyond it; but here a little old woman or crone was down on her hunkers, alongside a pail of water, and scrubbing away at the flagstones for dear life. I entered silently enough but she turned her head of a sudden, caught sight of me there – an imposing and unexpected figure – and let out a screech like a witch. On the instant there came a movement in one of the doors and Mrs. Gotobed appeared, saying, 'What is it,

Aggie?' and then rewarding me with a sour-faced look and a creaking of her stays. I said, 'Your pardon, ma'am. I'm trying to find my way to the stables; and your coachman, Buckle.'

Without moving she spoke over her shoulder, 'Mr. Gotobed'; and he came out behind her again looking as if he was about to start wringing his hands but still not quite getting so far. 'If you'll follow me, sir,' he answered.

'These'll be your quarters?' I asked.

With one eye on his wife, very likely because two would have been over painful, he replied, 'Our parlour; and the pantry and silver room.' Next to this was a more than ordinary strong door with a heavy lock, and when I looked at that he added uncertainly, 'The wine cellar.'

'And that's always a place of interest to any right thinking man,' I remarked.

'Not these days,' madam cut in sharply. 'His lordship's stocks are somewhat running down. Mr. Gotobed will take you to the stables.'

So I followed him out meekly and we passed round the back of the house into the stable yard, where I noted another entrance; most likely into the kitchens.

We discovered Buckle in the harness room, with my post boy seated on an upturned pail and gossiping. Him I dismissed with a jerk of the head and an instruction to have my chaise ready directly and my clerk waiting; and then said to the other, 'Well, Buckle, you'll have heard by now who I am. And by the look of you you're a man of few and short words like me. So let's have none wasted.'

'It will be about his lordship?' he asked.

'It will not,' I cut him short. 'We're satisfied about

63

him. That was your mate, Thomas Godsave.'

'No mate of mine,' he grunted. 'Wicked little bastard, for all his quiet ways.'

'We'll hang him yet,' I promised. 'For now I want an account of the highway robbery. How it was you got back here so late? Well after dark.'

The fellow scratched his head with an air of considering this. 'Was late starting. Ladyship kept us waiting best part of the morning while she made her farewells. Then they sent a groom to come as far as Kingston, but his hoss cast a shoe t'other side of Esher.'

'It did cast a shoe? How long did that hold you up?'

He stared at me. 'To be sure it cast'n. I got down myself to have a look. As for holding up, ladyship were in a tearing hurry by then; she says to drive on and be damned.'

'And what then? Which way did you come?'

'Godsave should've met us by the White Lion at Kingston. Her warn't there and ladyship says to drive on again. Lit the lamps up to Gallus Hill, come along by Richmond Park, bear left at Earl of Bessborough's lands, turn at the King's Head and through Roehampton to Cut Throat Lane.'

'Where did the highwayman stop you?'

''Bout midway along Cut Throat. Chose his place well, the villain. It was black dark, and there the bastard was, come out of the trees, crying "Stand and deliver".'

I studied him carefully. A big lump of a man like most of these coachmen and, you would think, handy with his whip; likewise, if I was any judge, as stubborn as a donkey. I said, 'Thomas Godsave?'

'Thomas Godsave for sure,' he answered.

64

'You recognised him, though it was black dark?'

'Was a bit of light from the lamps. I knowed him right enough. I said, "What be you up to, Thomas Godsave?"'

'Did you see his face?'

He grunted. 'Head was covered with a bag. But I knowed'n. He were holding the pistol in's left hand. Godsave's caggy handed.'

'Holding the pistol,' I said. 'One pistol. And you were carrying no armament yourself?' He shook his head and I asked, 'You didn't think to cut him across the face with your whip and drive on. You're a big fellow.'

'No matter how big you be you're none the better of a pistol ball in your belly.'

'You're a wise man,' I observed. 'Now, what about his horse?'

'Never seen it before; hired hack by the look of it. Must've took a hoss from our stables to let on he were coming to Kingston and picked up this other somewhere. Our animal were a dapple grey and he must've turned her loose for she came back to the stable herself. Reckon he done that so's nobody should know the hoss. He'm a tricky cunning little rascal.'

I pondered that, concluded it was not of much weight for the present, and then said, 'So after the robbery you drove on none the worse.'

'Except ladyship got the vapours; had to help her out of the carriage when we come back here. For all that there was a right tantivy as she told his lordship. Then he had me in and cussed me up hill and down dale. Swore I was in league with Godsave.'

'And was you?'

The fellow turned surly at that. 'I don't aim to get

my neck cricked, master. Anyway I couldn't put up with the sight of the little bastard. Cunning as a fox and artful in his ways at getting round the women. He knowed what he was about.'

'That's for certain,' I agreed. 'This affair's been planned these several months past. What's he like to look at?'

'Stocky chap, but terrible strong. Fresh faced and blue eyes. Let on to be ready to do anything for anybody but always had his own reasons for it; specially with ladyship.'

'A regular little villain,' I said. 'I know the sort. Now, Buckle; say he's hiding up about here, which I fancy he is, where d'you guess it might be?'

Yet again he scratched his head. 'Well now, that's a question. Not the gipsies, for he were always fearful of their queen, Mrs. Shanko; reckoned she could put the dark eye on you. Nor yet the tinkers. He fell foul of them over summat, and they'd cut his lights out if they got the chance. And the Green Man's careful of highwaymen on account the last landlord got hanged for sheltering one not twelve months back. He'd most like try the inn by the telegraph. They'm game for anything, that lot.'

I continued to regard this fine fellow – who, to tell the truth, seemed in no way uneasy – and asked, 'What d'you know about a certain Captain Roderick Medfield?'

He stared again and then grinned at me slyly. 'Cap'n Roddy? He'm a roaring boy, that one.'

'So I'm told on all sides. When was he seen about here last?'

His look was somewhat more cunning still. 'In the summer; July time. I recollect that well, for he were

66

rolling my lady's maid in the hay loft. A high-nosed trollop, that one, but not over particular where she took her oats.'

'He's not been seen since?'

'Not so far as I know. And I'd have heard of'n you can be sure.'

He seemed to be telling the truth, though you must never believe these rogues, and I said, 'There's one more question. What were you doing last night? Between ten o'clock and half gone eleven?'

'Why, in here throwing dice,' he answered. 'Along with Nicholas Trott, the first groom and Hack.' I misliked the look on his face; there was something here for certain, but he added, 'And they'll tell you the same.'

'So you couldn't have seen anything of Godsave. And maybe that's just as well, for there's no doubt he did for my lord out of revenge, because the poor gentleman laid an information against him. So you'll do well to remember that you identified him first; and wise to keep close and look to yourself after dark if he's still lurking hereabouts.' But again I had the fancy that there was something there, that he did not look so taken aback as I should have expected. Thinking that I'd have it out of him yet, but let him rest for now, I asked one last question. 'How many pistols did you say Tom Godsave was carrying?'

'I told you,' he answered. 'One to be sure. In's left hand.'

'Then bear in mind that he still has it. And for your own safety if you get the breath or a smell of where he's hiding come and tell me fast.'

So I went on my way, not displeased; musing on the difference between two pistols and one, and reflecting as I passed round to the front of the house that it would have been a very fair establishment better looked after. My post chaise was ready for me with the boy standing by his horses and the little rascal Maggsy waiting; and, as I cocked an eye up, Sir Tobias standing in one of the first floor windows looking down at me – that would be my lady's parlour, no doubt. I doffed my hat to him genteelly and, thinking that a little further mystification might well add to his interest in the art and science of detection, I continued on past the steps and pillars of the entrance looking for the window with a pane of broken glass.

The snow here was smooth and clean, a rarely pretty sight and a pity to disturb, but I set to raking in it with the tip of my cane. As I expected, I turned up one sliver of glass and then two or three more and bending down, not without a certain small puffing, I perceived that they were all lying snug with some inches of snow beneath them and more again above. 'So ho,' I said, well content, and then picked my way daintily back to the post chaise; noting that Sir Tobias was still watching, doffing my hat again and this time bowing lest the lady should be close behind him and in need of greeting.

'The hosses're getting cold,' the post boy observed.

'So we'll warm 'em with a touch of exercise,' I answered. 'And you'll be the better of a quart of ale to wet your whistle. We'll take a turn as far as the inn by the new telegraph.'

'This'll cost you a pretty penny afore you've done,' he said.

'Prettier still when you get it,' I told him. 'Be damned to your impudence. Get on your way, boy; you're about the business of our Sovereign Lord the

King, and the justice of His Realm.'

That cowed the rogue and we started out, with Maggsy jigging up and down like a dwarf on a whore's belly and crowing, 'Ain't this the life; this suits me proper. They said his lordship made the most horrible corpse ever, they said his eyeballs was hanging out on his cheeks, but I told 'em not so because I seen 'em throttled before and it's the tongue comes out, the same as if they get hanged slow instead of dropping; and . . .'

Here I took my cane to him and silenced the dreadful creature, saying, 'D'you recollect what I told you about sitting quiet and minding your manners and listening? Who was there and what did you hear?'

He fell into a fit of sulks but said, 'There was a big fat woman they called Mrs. Peascod, she was the cook. And that one who met us, Mr. Hack. And a middling-sized girl chopping up turnips and a little'n scouring out the pots; they was both snivelling but enjoying it. Then there was a boy come in with a load of wood for the oven. This Mrs. Peascod'd been nipping at the gin – I seen 'em like that before – and she was rolling dough and laughing and weeping and dropping her tears in it. And Mr. Hack said his lordship'd be glad of that, it'd save the salt. That set her off in another howl.'

'Come to it,' I said impatiently. 'What did they say?'

'I'm atelling you. The boy reckoned there was somebody sneaking about gone eleven last night, which he heard on account of coming down to lie by the kitchen fire, him freezing stiff in the garret. And Mr. Hack says if he did hear anything he'd best keep his trap shut unless he wanted to get his gullet squeezed too; and if

he'd wanted to keep warm he'd have done best to rollick Poll, who was well known to be hot enough for two.
That was the middling girl, because she flourished the
knife at him and screeched if she got much of that talk
she'd cut his liver out, and when she fancied a rollicking it'd be with somebody better than a flea-bit hall
boy; and maybe she would if they all got turned away
over this, it'd be a brighter life than chopping turnips.'

'So far,' I observed, 'you've told me nothing of any
account. Except it's a most ungenteel household.'

'Very snug I reckoned it was,' he answered. 'After
that Hack got fetched out by the one as looks like an
undertaker's weeping man, and then they went on
again about being turned away if the house got shut
up. At this Mrs. Peascod lets fall another flood of tears
and says it's well known that her ladyship'd as soon
burn the place down as look at it, and the first chance
she gets she'll be off with Sir Tobias. So then Poll
answers that it won't go to her anyway, it'll go to
somebody named Master Roderick, who it seems is a
roaring soldier. And Mrs. Peascod weeps that'll be
worse 'cause he'll gamble it all away and them with it.
Upon which the little girl spoke up, crying that if
Master Roderick comes here there won't be a wench in
the village safe; and Poll gives a laugh and screeches
that'll be something to look forward to anyway while
it lasts. I reckon she's only got her mind on one thing,
and it ain't chopping turnips neither.'

'Be so good to keep your moral observations to
yourself,' I ordered him. 'And then?'

'Then Mrs. Peascod says the title will go to Master
Roderick, but his lordship'd never leave him the
property, such as it is, because he hates the sight of
him. And that Poll says "No? So what was him and her

70

ladyship hollering and yellocking at each other about in my lord's study last night? And what have they been yellocking about on and off ever since the jewels got pinched?" '

'Maggsy,' said I, 'you're a smart little rascal. And could I but get at my purse I'd give you a silver sixpence.'

'I never had sixpence all my own before,' he answered.

'Let us keep to your report,' I told him, somewhat testily.

'Well then, Hack come back after a time. Seem's Hack didn't fancy you all that much.' The boy looked at me sidelong. 'He says you was a right old strutting gander and he'd admire to get his carving knife up your arse after cooking you an hour or two on the spit.'

I am a man of profound control, and to this I said nothing, but resolved on another discourse with Master Hack before long. 'Continue,' I instructed the boy.

'They got on about Godsave. Mrs. Peascod took another swig at the gin and slopped some on the dough in mistake for water and asks does Hack reckon he done it, and Hack says it don't matter much, one man's as good as another to a thief taker and they're bound to make an example for throttling a lord, 'case everybody takes to doing it like they did in France.' He paused for breath, being somewhat in need of it, and added, 'I wisht I'd seen that revolution. Must've been better'n a Newgate hanging.'

I gave him a light cut with my cane, just smart enough to discourage such improper sentiments, and with another touch of sulks he went on, 'Mrs. Peascod does another weep, and Poll says she don't think Godsave done it 'cause he'd never have had the spirit, he never even had the spirit to let her know what he'd got inside his breeches; and then the little'n spoke up again. She said he might if her ladyship asked him to, 'twas well known he'd lie down and let her ladyship trample over his back if he thought she'd fancy it.'

'So ho,' I said. 'Continue again, boy.'

'Wasn't much more. They got to talking about where Godsave was hiding, and all reckoned it was somewhere hereabouts on account of coming back last night to throttle his lordship; upon which Mrs. Peascod sets up another howl and screeches they'll all be murdered in their beds before long, and Hack answers that she'd best give over opening the yard door at night for Buckle to come in and roll her when he's feeling randy. Then the post boy puts his head in to say I was to come and be ready for you.'

'You've done well, boy,' I said. 'And I'm particular pleased.'

'You couldn't see your way to making it a shillun?' he asked, 'when you can get at your purse.'

Fortunately the matter was brought to a happy conclusion because upon that we reached the inn. A rough place though bigger than I expected, squatting low and dark under the trees with the snow about it trodden to a pissy mush; a stack of firewood to one side and a cattle pen, and beyond it a huddle of skin tents and bothies. It looked a house fit for any villainy, and I descended from the chaise to view it with some disfavour before passing on to the encampment behind, picking my way delicately through the filth. Here there was a drab suckling a child in one hovel, in one more a fellow who addressed me with a tongue so outlandish I did not understand a word of it. But save for a few miserable bits and rags of possessions the others was empty, and no sign of Thomas Godsave; so I turned back to the inn itself where Maggsy and the post boy were awaiting me impatiently.

The rogues within was singing lustily; and as we approached the door I stopped short, for they were bawling that canting, villainous thieves kitchen doggerel of which I have already spoken.

'Oh, dark and dismal was the day when last I see my Meg;
She'd a government band around each hand
And another one round each leg.
And another one round each leg, my lads,
As the big ship left the bay;
Oh, do you think she'll remember me ten thousand miles away?
Sing ho, my lads, sing hey, my lads,
Where the dancing dolphins play,
And the whales and sharks are up to their larks
Ten thousand miles away.'

But I am a man not lightly daunted and with the other two at my heels I thrust open the door. It was a low dirty hole with timber beams and daubed plaster, the first black and the other yellow with smoke, poor bottle glass windows and dull pewter, but a good roaring fire; that being one way these country savages never stint themselves, having plenty of wood around. There was a dozen or more rude fellows sitting at the tables and settles in a stink of damp frieze, cattle and liquor, and bellowing the chorus of that damned song to a little peg-legged rascal scraping at a fiddle; however, it died away as we entered and they fell silent,

73

gazing at us as if genteel company was no very common thing here. But the landlord was civil enough, he said, 'Good day to you, gentlemen; what can I have the pleasure?'

'For me a pint of hot rum toddy,' I commanded, 'for my clerk the same of small beer.' And marking the post boy with his tongue very near hanging out, I added, 'And a quart of ale.'

'Hot, with nutmeg and sugar,' the hardy rogue put in.

I looked at him sideways; that would cost me another ha'penny. The expenses of this affair were already counting up to a pretty detail and it was worse when that little rascal Maggsy piped up, 'Me too.'

But I took it bravely, saying, 'What they fancy. That was a hearty song you were about. But I'd have thought more suitable to Rochester than Putney.'

'We get many travelling men,' the landlord answered, 'and Little Peggy here's got nimble fingers for a good tune.'

'Bit of music, sir,' this Little Peggy chimed in. 'Poor man's pleasure; pretty near the only one we got.'

'Come now,' I told him good humouredly, 'you've a snug roof above your head, a good fire and a pot in your hand.'

The rogue scraped a chord on his fiddle, doing a sort of shuffle dance with his wooden leg. 'Asking your grace, not all that often. I seen some terrible times. Forty years at sea, sir, and lost me leg in a fearful storm off the Coromandel Coast.'

'And no doubt with some fine tales to tell,' I said, turning again to the landlord and counting the coins out of my purse. 'I'll have your best rum.'

The other rogues were nudging and whispering

between themselves, plainly set to make a fool out of this gentleman stranger as these country savages love to do, but they fell silent as I said that, while the landlord himself paused about putting the ale to mull. Then that pestilential fiddler was at my elbow, along with a great hulking fellow beside him, and whining, 'A pot of warm beer for a poor man, your grace?'

It did not please me, the more so as the others was snickering and whispering again, but I nodded to the landlord and asked, 'D'you ever have any of my Lord Hartingfield's men come drinking here?'

There was a silence again before he answered, 'We've heard of doings at Hartingfield that're no affair of ours. We want no part of 'em. If I might be so bold, sir, what's your business?'

'Well now,' I answered, 'as to that, I'm a writer to *The Gentleman's Magazine* sent out here to make an enquiry and report on the recent highway robbery. It's a rare story in London, I can tell you. All the clubs are buzzing with it.' I winked at the man. 'And not without a good laugh on the quiet.'

His face went as wooden as his counter, and the others as quiet. 'A writing gentleman, sir? Well that's wonderful learned; but we don't reckon a lot on such stuff here, we likes to sit quiet and keep our noses clean.' He placed the two pots of ale and my rum toddy on the counter and finished, 'Likewise the other matter you speak of took place a mile or more away, and that's far enough for honest folk to mind their own business.'

The fiddler was plucking at my sleeve. 'Play a tune for your grace?' he fawned, ' "The Spanish Ladies" or "Way Down Hilo" or a little jig? We likes a little jig.'

75

'Not now, my man,' I answered, 'I'm in conversation.'

'Now then,' the big lout beside him spoke up, 'I'll not see poor Peggy put down so.'

'You'll hold your tongue,' I told him, and went on to the landlord, 'There's many a blind dog smells enough. I daresay I could find half a gold guinea for any man who can furnish information touching the present whereabouts of this Thomas Godsave.'

'No, master,' the bully said again, 'you've wounded poor Peggy's nice feelings; you'll buy him a pot of rum for solace; with one for me to keep him company.'

'I'll buy you a cut with my cane for better manners,' I answered. 'What kind of a house is this, landlord?'

'Maybe it's your manners they don't fancy,' he said.

This time it was the post boy plucking at me, whispering, 'Come out of it. Can't you see they're shaping for a fight? I'll not have you killed before you pay me what you owe.'

Even then all might have passed off had not the fiddler – who was plainly over ripe for the gallows and for certain mistaking the nature of my horrible little monster from his genteel clothes – made a cruel, lewd and indecent snatch at Maggsy. At this the boy set up a wicked screech, struck the fellow heartily where it was likely to do him a mischief, and sank his teeth into the whining little rogue's forearm. Whereupon the bully let out a roar and raised a pewter pot which would surely have laid Maggsy dead had it struck him, and had I not first presented the savage a sharp slash across his face with my cane.

You shall note that in such a situation if they rush you at once, which they will if you show sign of fear, you are outnumbered and done and can only fight

your way out as best you may; but if you show resolute
they will just as often brindle and hackle like mongrel
dogs firing their courage. This they did now, only
while the bully was nursing his cheek, but long
enough for me to shrug out of my top coat and capes
with a purposeful air and hand Maggsy my cane,
saying, 'Have a care to that, it was given me as a
present by His Majesty.' This also gave them pause for
another moment. The post boy had taken himself off,
and I thought that was the way of such wherever you
met them; but in this I misjudged him, as you shall
see.

The landlord was not over set on the business and
he cried, 'Let be, Jem; we shall have trouble of this.'
But that touched the fellow off and he swept the
fiddler aside and came at me snarling. Better than half
a stone heavier than me and with a long reach, but the
clod wasn't to know that before now I'd done my turn
or two in a friendly way with Black Tinman, the London pugilist; a one-time tin miner and a wicked fighter
who'd taught me a trick or two. The first swing with a
fist like a hand of pork I slipped under and planted a
sharp rap on his nose to start with – for any of the
ladies who might ever find themselves in such a situation shall note that there's nothing so discommodes a
man as blood and snot running down his chaps – and
then came round with a hard hook in his kidneys.
That steadied the rogue. But it wasn't him I was so
concerned about as the others; one of 'em howled
'Give Jemmy room, boys', and they'd be content
enough so long as they thought he was going to make
bone jelly of me, but at the first sign that he was getting the worst of it I should have the whole pack on
my hands together with sticks, cudgels and very likely

a knife or two.

However, one wind at a time as my sea captain says, and I moved my head aside to let a hearty swipe pass and repeated my former attack with certain differences; first closing his right eye for him and on the instant following with a pile driver in the pit of his belly. But I wasn't to have it all my own way, nor was it a mill to be conducted by Jack Broughton's London Prize Ring Rules; my blows had enraged more than hurt him, and if the poor fool had little science he'd brute strength enough to make up for it. We went at it ding dong until more by luck than judgement he fetched me a buffet to the side of my head which rattled my teeth, and then brought up his knee in a dastardly stroke at my most sensitive parts. Only by flinging myself back did I escape a fearful mischief, and in this moment when he had the passing advantage he swept up a quart pot from the counter with his fist inside it, a truly frightful weapon.

Drove back in a corner I was hard put to; and the others was closing round for the kill, making the snarling outcry of their kind. But at that instant my post boy returned just within the door and carrying his whip. He bawled 'Stand back, God damn you; I'll not see him killed before he pays me what he owes. Stand back, or I'll have the faces off you!' That daunted them, for a coachman's whip is an ugly thing properly used, and likewise it distracted bully Jem's attention for just long enough. Saying, 'If that's the way you want it, my lad,' I fetched a crippling blow to his guts and as he whooped for breath little Maggsy, not to be outdone, dashed a pot of hot ale in his face. On the instant, for all he caught me a glancing blow with his own pot, I went in for a hard one two three; the first at his nose once more, what was left of it, the second a left-handed jab to his belly again, and the last a most clean and pretty upward swing at his chin. The wonder of it was that it didn't break his neck. He went down like a felled ox and not being in any mood for niceties I seized him by the hair, gave his head a smart rap on the flagstones to make sure of him, and then stepped back. I was breathing a trifle hard.

'Well,' the landlord said, 'thank God it was no worse. You shouldn't a picked a quarrel.'

'There was no quarrel picked,' I told him 'and you know it,' while the post boy cried, 'Come out now; afore you start trouble.'

'All in good time,' I answered. 'Use your whip if you must, give these rogues a foretaste of what they're like to get,' and turned back on the landlord saying, 'Now have this plain. I want information touching Thomas Godsave. If I get it before nightfall we'll call that a good hearty mill and say no more about it. But if I don't I'll see you and this lot on the Rochester hulks for a few years; and very likely a flogging or two for make weight. Make up your mind, my man.'

'We don't have no information,' he grunted.

'Then you'd best get some,' I said settling my beaver with a smart slap and taking my capes and cane from Maggsy. 'I mean to know whether Godsave's on the heath or not, so if you want to save yourself you'll find out. And if you're uneasy who I am you'd best ask Sir Tobias Westleigh when next you see him.' With that I marched out pretty well pleased with myself and little the worse for the adventure; this being a fortunate thing since I'd a mind to go social calling later that day.

'Well,' the post boy observed, 'you're a fine game

cock, master, my God you are,' while young Maggsy chimed in, 'A rare wicked fighter. They'll have your tripes out for that, they'll have your tripes out the first chance they gets. My eye, this is the life, this is; while it lasts.'

'I'll have none of your impudence, neither of you,' I told them, getting into the chaise. 'You may take me back to such civilisation as the King's Head can offer; we'll leave these heathens to lick their wounds.'

Once again I was not ill satisfied. It is ever my habit to strike down two birds with one stone, and I had now made it clear that I was not a man to be trifled with, while at the same event saving myself a vast deal of trouble scouring and searching this damnation heath; there being little doubt that our rascally landlord would set his boys about that for the sake of his own skin. I had only three other matters to consider. Whether those rogues had set about me as any savages will always attack their betters, given the chance; whether our fine, sporting Sir Tobias had put them up to it; or whether a messenger had ridden fast across the heath from Hartingfield. Either of those last two might well mean that some person, known or unknown, was becoming fearful that I was sniffing too close to the truth. But it was of no great importance at this present. Time, I reflected, would bring the answer; time and Jeremy Sturrock.

V

It was gone three when I set out again, about the time I judged a widow woman would be solacing her loneliness with a dish of tea by a bright fire and inclined for company. On some reflection I had kept the post boy and chaise with me – not without considering how fast the expenses of this affair were mounting, but persuading myself that one way or another I could still contrive to meet them and yet leave myself a few guineas in pocket – for there was no other conveyance save open horseback in this benighted village. So, having given Master Maggsy certain instructions concerning Mistress Bet and other matters at the King's Head, I left him behind to see to them, and set out on my social occasions. And for these a post chaise, although not precisely a private carriage, would still preserve a better gentility than plodding through the snow on foot like a countryman.

We came to a most pretty, tidy cottage. A trim white fence and beyond that a garden where the widow would grow her gilly flowers and pinks in summer but now hummocked in snow, a fancy porch in the countrified fashion, and bay windows one each side with a comfortable gleam of firelight in them. I beat a polite rap on the knocker, not like the peremptory tattoo of the law, and near enough on the instant the door was opened by a maid as pretty and trim as the cottage itself. She bobbed and smiled up at me, and I said, 'Me dear, Mr. Jeremy Sturrock of London, bidden to wait upon Mistress Quince by an old sea captain friend of her late husband.' You shall note that the ladies can never resist mention of a sea captain.

The child whispered, 'Please to wait, sir,' and vanished; but it was not long before she was back doing another bob and saying, 'Please to step this way, sir.'

She led me through a little hall not a lot bigger than herself into a snug parlour with white panelling, needlework covers, furniture after the manner of Mr. Chippendale, a bright clear fire and a copper kettle on the hearth. There the Widow Quince was standing to await me, likewise as neat and trim as her parlour itself. I have always been most partial to a ripe, warm widow and unless I was much mistaken this was of the ripest and warmest; buxom, but not overly so, a merry face and bright eyes with a glint of mischief in them, and plainly nobody's fool. It must have been a sad thing for poor Mr. Quince to go on his dark journey and leave such a comforting morsel behind, and I did my most genteel bow, announcing, 'Ma'am, your particular obedient servant; and asking your pardon for this intrusion.'

'An old sea captain friend?' said she. 'I don't recall but one. Would that be Captain Spadduck of the West Indies trade?'

'The same, ma'am,' I answered. 'And at present most splenetic that this pestilential war with the French is upsetting a peaceful sailorman's affairs. Nonetheless he bids me assure you of his most excellent regards.'

'Then, sir,' she says, 'you have the advantage of me. For my dear late husband was a corn chandler of Sheen and never got nearer the sea in his life than Richmond Bridge.'

I am not easily at a loss for words; a man who has

dealt comfortably with many a villain and many a wicked situation. But here I was silenced; and deeply shocked that such a pretty and obliging woman could descend so low. Now here is a moral observation, addressed above all to the ladies. Put not your trust in deceit, for it will surely be your downfall; especially when dealing with an officer of the law. But I made the best of it, saying, 'I ask your pardon for the subterfuge...'

She interrupted me, laughing merrily, the wanton creature. 'Fiddlesticks, sir, we all know who you are. You're that thief taker, come to catch poor Tom Godsave and hang him for forty pounds. News spreads fast in Roehampton, sir.'

'Ma'am,' I answered with dignity, 'I am not of that sort. My concern is to uphold the law; and to call upon all true subjects of His Majesty, God bless him, to assist me in the same. As for Thomas Godsave, as I see it at this moment there are some as might be trying to hang him, but I am not one of them.'

She gazed at me consideringly. 'I will say you're not as I'd thought a thief taker to be. A monster with a villainous face and a growth of beard on his chin; carrying a great bunch of manacles, a red weskit, pistols in his belt and all.'

'Such, ma'am,' I assured her somewhat stiffly, 'is not the modern fashion among officers of Bow Street.'

She laughed again, merrier than ever. 'Tut, sir, climb down off your high horse, for I'm a teasing creature. And tell me,' she whispered, 'is it true that my Lord Hartingfield was done to death and murdered?'

'It is indeed,' I answered, 'and a pretty piece of villainy.'

'Well,' she breathed, 'what does the world come to? Though there's few about here who'll regret him. Least of all her ladyship and a certain baronet of this parish, though a gentleman we all have a vast admiration for. Come, sir, I'll send for your driver to warm himself in the kitchen while we settle to a dish of tea.'

So it turned out better than it started and, true as Backus had said, she was rare prattler; the more so I judged for the pleasure of having a man about the place after long abstinence, and a man of consequence above these dull country fellows. Indeed when I let slip by accident that I was companion and bodyguard to His Majesty nothing would satisfy her but talk about St. James's and Kew House, our poor king's melancholic affliction, and the doings of His Royal Highness. Seeing that I was making a notable impression on the dear soul I humoured her for a time as a gentleman should, but at last brought back the discourse to this present affair. I let her have her head and satisfied her curiosity to the full on my Lord Hartingfield's tragic end and then said, 'I will observe, ma'am, that for a peer of the realm it's a strange household.'

'Strange?' she echoed. 'It's a disgrace. And this such an elegant and genteel district.' I considered privately that there might be several opinions about that, but she continued, 'With our Earl of Bessborough to one side and several other notable gentlemen in Putney, Sir Tobias hard by, and dear Mrs. Siddons herself residing at Bristol House near the Bowling Green. I say it's a disgrace, sir. Such unmannerly servants; and those Gotobeds. Depend upon it, if they were turned away from Hartingfield they'd never find another place, for none would have them.'

Stemming this cataract I said, 'Yet my lady herself seems most stylish; and of the high French aristocracy, as I understand.'

My widow contrived to look dark and mysterious. 'That was a marriage of convenience. You've heard how she was left alone in '93? Well then, there were plenty of beaux in London after her, but a shade too dashing, if you take me; and she a notably shrewd woman. So she chose a near enough elderly man who told her that he was like to die soon. No doubt hoping to find herself free once more and replace the titles she'd lost in France with another gained in England. And it's said that my lord used pretty near the last of his resources about the town house in Hill Street to ensnare her.'

'Well,' I mused, 'shrewd she certainly was. For my lord did die soon after all.'

The Widow Quince gazed at me, one hand at her breast, whispering, 'No. Mr. Sturrock, you're not saying that my lady . . .'

'I'm not saying nothing,' I answered. 'She didn't do it herself, that's for sure. It takes a fair amount of strength to throttle a man, and my lady don't have the build.'

This time she let out a little scream, saying, 'No!' again. 'I'll not believe it, Mr. Sturrock. Not Sir Toby?'

'Come, ma'am,' I advised, 'don't let's over run the course. I'm only observing that such things have been known. Tell me now, for I'm sure you know, how is it the estate's so impoverished?'

'Ah,' she said, on happier ground, 'that was the last lordship. Uncle to this one, and a most notorious rake and profligate. He was shot in a duel up here on the heath – it was an affair of some Covent Garden dancer – having gambled most of the fortune away. So this lord, or who was this lord, poor soul, came into the title and Hartingfield and the town house with scarce enough money to keep them up.'

'And I've heard,' I prompted her, 'that the next Lord Hartingfield is very near as bad.'

'Captain Medfield? Oh, a rogue, sir; a regular riotous rogue. But he'll only take the title, for the property must surely go to my lady; no doubt what she had her eye to. And lucky for those rascally servants, and in particular the Gotobeds; for the captain would turn them away at an hour's notice. Not but what my lady will no doubt make some changes,' she prattled on gaily.

'A mysterious household,' I observed. 'And, I fancy, very different from Sir Tobias Westleigh's.'

'Monstrous different,' she cried warmly. 'My own little girl Ginny's sister is in service at Westleigh House under Mrs. Peggit. A very nice little situation and a most proper woman in a well conducted establishment.'

'For all Sir Toby's said to be something of a sportsman?'

She bridled a little at that. 'My dear soul, we like a man to take his pleasures like a man; so long as they're natural pleasures. Sir Toby's most highly thought of here. Indeed we were all near enough desolated a few months back when there was talk of him settling on his estate in Scotland.'

I finished my tea genteelly, not over fond of it though I happen to know that their Majesties will often sit together and take a dish with pleasure, and repeated, 'His estate in Scotland?'

'It came to him through his mother. Old Sir Tobias married a Scots lady; a very ancient family, and most beautiful, if you ever see her portrait at the house by Mr. Gainsborough. The estate was settled on her and Sir Toby still holds it, and Lavinia Peggit was in a rare taking when he said that he was of a mind to retire up there for a year or two. But no more's been heard of it since, so most likely it's all blown over. Lord, how do I rattle on,' she cried. 'My dear late Mr. Quince always used to say that, before he passed away and left me inconsolable.'

'Ma'am,' I said, 'if I can be so bold, there's never no reason for a woman so ripe and bountiful as yourself to remain that way.'

'You're very kind,' she returned. 'And I'll not deny that when my poor Quince was lying on his last bed he told me "Amelia, my love, don't stint yourself. Look on it as an act of Christian charity and make some other man as comfortable as you've made me." So far I haven't had the heart, but I can feel my time coming on.'

'And something more than Christian charity, ma'am,' I said. 'A snugger situation for some fortunate fellow I never did see.'

'He'd have to be a man of the world, Mr. Sturrock. A man of wider interests than Roehampton village. I dearly love a rich gossip about Society and Royalty. Though to tell the truth there have been times when I've thought of Mr. Backus.'

'You'd consider Landlord Backus a reliable man, would you, ma'am? One to keep himself out of trouble?'

'Why to be sure. And the King's Head's a warm house. It'd suit me nicely to have the management of that.'

'I doubt you'd find the girl Bet a bit of a handful.

Did you ever hear that she's tossing her ribbons at this Tom Godsave?'

'My dear soul,' She laughed at me again. 'The whole village knows it. And a very proper match. I heard even that her ladyship'd do something for the pair of 'em if anything ever came of it. But that was before this dreadful happening,' she sighed. 'Only the dear Lord knows how it'll end now.'

'Well enough, ma'am,' I promised her. 'But Bet's a handsome wench. I'd have thought she might look higher for herself. A second groom; and not over bright, so I'm told.'

'A good obedient husband when trained properly,' she said. 'And Bet'll see to that as soon as she gets him into bed.'

'But simple. Why I've heard that he's fearful of some queen of the gipsies here; some Mrs. Shanko.'

'As who wouldn't be?' Widow Quince demanded. 'Look now what happened to Farmer Knatchbull over Wimbledon. The gipsies was taking too many of his hares, which he was reasonable about for the most part, but in the end he rode up the heath and gave 'em a right round cursing. And Mrs. Shanko sat on the steps of her wagon watching him, and at last she said "Save your breath, farmer, for you'll have need of it before long." Well then, not twenty four hours after the poor soul was struck by a seizure in the very act of sitting on his own chamber pot, and from that moment said never another word until he died. Consider the indignity of it.'

'Pooh, ma'am,' I said, 'It's a natural hazard. But Tom Godsave wouldn't go anywhere near the gipsies even if he needed a horse?'

'He would not,' she answered. 'Nor any other right

minded person.'

'Was there ever anything between him and my lady's one time maid?' I asked.

'That high nosed trollop? She called herself Mademoiselle Clarice d'Arbois. Why, bless you sir, she wouldn't have looked at him. Do you know,' the widow cried, 'what I've heard reported she said of us Roehampton people? You'll not believe it. She said we was a lot of low, country savages.'

'Well!' I answered, breathtaken. 'The impudence of that. It's the French,' I added. 'They're all inclined that way.' My Widow Quince looked riper and warmer than ever in her indignation, and the firelight made it look darker beyond the window. I was loath to leave but there was a few flakes of snow starting to fall once more and no doubt that surly post boy would be complaining that his horses were getting cold again. Moreover there was business yet to do so I rose up, however unwillingly, saying, 'A most proper entertainment, and a more than agreeable discourse. Your most obedient servant, ma'am.'

'No doubt I'm a forward woman,' she observed, 'but it'd be laughable for me to fancy myself a blushing maid at my age. You'll visit again, Mr. Sturrock?'

'Ma'am,' I assured her, 'it'll be constantly in my thoughts. I've no great mind for blushing maidens neither.'

So we parted the best of friends, with a promise of more to come, and I returned to the King's Head pondering over the morsels of information my widow had let slip in her prattle; nothing much, yet enough to satisfy nearly all of my suspicions. Arriving there I was turning into the parlour as Landlord Backus appeared from his snug, carrying a dirty scrap of paper and eyeing it and myself with about equal disfavour. He announced, 'This was brought for you a quarter hour since. And I'll thank you to keep that wicked little whelp you've taken up with under proper control. I'll tell you, Mr. Sturrock, I'm of two minds whether to turn the pair of you out of my house this instant.'

With more than a notion of what the trouble was about I told him mildly, 'You'll be most unwise if you do, Mr. Backus, for everybody's sake. What's the rascal been up to? And where is he?'

'A sneaking and prying all over the place,' Backus answered, 'no doubt with an eye to seeing what he can pilfer. He's in the stables now, where he belongs. We don't like his kind here, Mr. Sturrock, nor yours either come to that, and if you don't . . .'

'Have done,' I interrupted. 'If Maggsy's been in mischief he shall answer for it. Send him to me and let's get it done with.' The landlord looked as if he was about to take it further and I added, 'I've weightier affairs on my mind, Mr. Backus.'

That silenced him, and he turned away somewhat uncertainly while I went in to the fire and candlelight to examine my paper. A curious missive and written most uncouth, but plain enough to show how far my threat that morning had gone home, for it said as follows. 'Sir, we now noes who you be and wants noe part of the matter you are about on. This to sware that sum of the boys has bin all over the heath from richmond Park to wimbledon all most like places and sware likewise there be no sine of T. Godsave nor has nobody seen him not tinkers nor gippoes. Also Jem now beeing of a broke head likwise swares he meant no harm only wishing a bit of teezing and if he had have noed who you was would not have come near. Praying the matter is now done with, obdt servint, Jos Lumkin.'

I was chuckling over this and resolving to preserve it for my memoirs when Backus came back bearing Maggsy with him by the scruff of his neck; the landlord flushed with the exercise and the boy kicking and cursing, giving by no means a bad account of himself, and with the beginnings of a ripe, shining black eye.

Not to be outmatched in curses Backus also expressed himself finely, and I told him, 'Have done,' again and then asked in an awful voice, 'Maggsy! What have you been up to?' The boy stared at me unbelieving with his one good eye and started, 'Well, God's truth, only what you ...' but I roared, 'Silence! I'll not be answered back to. Pray let me have him, Mr. Backus,' I continued, 'you shall watch me teach him manners.'

'Why, rot you,' Maggsy began again, but this I stopped with a smart slap and seized him by the scruff myself. Then I set to with my cane, not all that fierce but brisk enough to make him screech and yell; at the same time under cover of the uproar saying in his ear, 'Keep your mouth shut, you toad, or I'll lay on twice as hard.' He gave out most satisfying howls and I observed to Backus, 'It's a truly royal trouncing for that cane was presented to me by no less than His Majesty himself,' and at last asked, 'Now, sir, are you satisfied? For I'll warrant he is.' On the man intimating that he was, and also highly amused, I concluded. 'Then I'll ask you to send me in a quart of ale; for threshing the oats is always thirsty work.'

Laughing himself into a good humour again Backus left us, and Maggsy aimed a wicked kick at my shins which I dodged nimbly and replied to with a hearty shake to sober him. 'I wisht the devil may singe your breech for that,' he whimpered; 'I was only doing as you told me, and see what I get for it.'

'No, Maggsy,' I corrected him. 'Not for doing what I told you. For letting yourself get caught at it. And also to provide an air of righteousness. Observe that as a prime lesson in the art and science of detection; be ever righteous and never get caught. So an end to the snivelling; you're not hurt, and well you know it. Your report, Master Maggsy, and look sharp.' I silenced him again while they brought my ale in, let him have a good draught of it for solace, and then asked, 'Now then, did you search the place?'

'They was near enough chasing me by the end,' he admitted. 'But I reckon I looked everywhere. Wasn't no sign of hide nor hair of him. There's no Tom Godsave here, that's for certain.'

'So ho,' I mused. 'We're striking off his hiding places one by one. So what of the wench; our Bouncing Bet. And where did you get that shiner from?'

'She give it me. She'm a right wild cat that one; I'd as soon you hanged her as anybody.' I rattled the bottom of my tankard on the table and he went on hurriedly, 'Like you said I told her that his lordship was done for about eleven last night, and the coroner's going to bring it wilful murder against Thomas Godsave and he'll hang for sure unless them as knows how to find him come forward and say where he was at that time.'

'And what did she answer to that?'

'She tossed her curls at me and started "Sir Toby ..." but then changed her mind and says "Them as lives the longest'll see the most", and I said Tom Godsave for one won't live long enough to take a ride on her belly, and with that she come round with a back hander and give me this. I'd admire to see that bitch have a match with you,' he added. 'She'd put you down if anybody could.'

'You're a most horrible little monster,' I told him. 'Now be silent, for I wish to think.'

So we sat quiet by the fire until Sir Tobias arrived, with a sprinkle of snow on his capes for it was coming down thick again, when we took a pint of mulled claret apiece and settled to supper. Once more it was a very fair set out, a brace of ducks, a little sucking pig fancifully stuffed, and a salmon out of the river at Putney; somewhat commonplace but of a better flavour than you get in London where it's apt to be two or three days old before it reaches your table. The while I entertained him with an account of my adventure at the inn, keeping one eye on him to see how he took it. He looked at me sharpish, saying, 'I can teach these rogues manners if you wish.'

'Let it be,' I answered. 'I gave them a smart enough lesson. And I had some good out of it.'

He looked enquiring, but I did not choose to enlighten him and asked instead, 'There's one point, Sir Tobias; if I may be so bold. Those rascals was singing the same merry ditty as you favoured me with last night. What's your connection with that inn?'

He lifted his eyebrows at that and observed, 'By God, sir, you're impudent. But if you must know I'm training a man for a pugilist and we sometimes fight a practice bout there.'

'So that'll be another matter explained,' I said comfortably.

But we hadn't quite the same good company we

enjoyed last night, for Sir Tobias was plainly bent on business; he announced with uncommon sharpness, 'As Justice of this parish, sir, I feel obliged to say that I do not see you conducting this affair as I imagine a Bow Street officer should.'

'No, sir?' I asked, mildly enough. 'What would you have me do? Be out scouring the heath with a lantern?'

He had no answer to that, since there wasn't one, but he answered back, 'You may call it your new science of detection; but I've seen no activity save jaunts in your post chaise and questions which seem to have little bearing on the affair.'

'Activity is not always to be perceived, sir,' I said, tapping my forehead with the mouthpiece of my pipe. 'There's plenty going on up here. And if I may be ungenteel there's no profit to be gained by buzzing like a blue-arsed fly looking for a smell of honey.' I do not often indulge in rage unless there is something to be gained by it or unless my naturally choleric temper gives way, whichever comes the first. Therefore I took a draught of claret to calm myself, though feeling certain of my buttons straining at their moorings, and finished, 'It's only by this science we shall find the answer; by taking observation and putting such questions.'

'Then, sir,' he rejoined, 'permit me to say that you've asked enough. It's time for your conclusions.'

'And I'll ask more yet,' I promised him. 'I'll tell you some of 'em. First; why does one witness swear the highwayman is carrying one pistol while the other swears equally that he has two? Second; why does my lord's body look as if it was moved after death but before it stiffened; and if it was indeed, who moved it? Or another; why was the candles in my lord's cabinet not guttered though they must have been standing in a wicked draught from that open window, and why was the glass broke from it lying out in the snow instead of inside the room? Another again; what caused the bruise on my lord's forehead? One more, sir; why was my lord strangled when there was a knife lying there which would have killed him just as easy and quieter? And yet another; perhaps the most important of the lot; what was my lord writing when or before he was struck down, and where is it now? That's only a few of 'em,' I ended. 'But they'll do to be going on with. And what are the answers?'

'Lord, Mr. Sturrock,' Sir Tobias protested. 'I'm damned if I know. You fire a battery at me.'

'Aye, sir,' I answered, 'and it's a battery from which every shot'll tell before I'm done.'

He gave one of his short laughs at that but appeared to be somewhat moody now, gazing at the fire for a time before he said, 'There's one question you can answer me. You told that buzz fly Nokes that Hartingfield was killed between a quarter past ten and half after eleven. How d'you establish that?'

'Simple enough, sir, though I'm no physician. The body was frozen as stiff as a board, and must have been there for near enough twelve hours. Consider also the fire. By the look of the remains that was small enough to start with and the man, Hack, mended it at nine o'clock, while Gotobed testifies that it was burning through by a little beyond ten. No man in his senses, not even my lord, would remain sitting in that chamber with the cold as it was last night. My lord was wearing ordinary house clothes, you will recollect; even somewhat on the light side.'

'I applaud your observations,' Sir Tobias said, 'but is it important?'

'It is to the extent that if Godsave wants to save himself he must come forward and prove where he was at that time; and the other people with him.' Sir Tobias nodded to that, taking my point, and I continued, 'I'll confess I'm of two minds. Whether to wait for this to happen and so get at the truth of the highway robbery. Or whether to track down the true murderer of his lordship myself and let my lady's jewels go hang.'

You will note, I hope, that I was handling this situation with a nice, delicate diplomacy; and Sir Tobias himself was not unaware of it, for he gave another of his laughs and remarked, 'You'll permit me to mention that you're a man as finds a deal of pleasure in his own cleverness, Mr. Sturrock. Take care you don't over run it. Your duty's clear.'

'I fear it is,' I agreed. 'And duty's often a bitter load. Does not Mr. Wordsworth make some such remarkably heavy handed observations on the same subject? Come,' I cried, 'that's enough of business. We had a good merry evening last night; why not another?'

'I thank you, sir,' he answered, 'but I'm not of the mood. And I've matters of my own to attend to.' And with that he left us.

You may scarcely believe it, but during all this colloquy Master Maggsy had sat quite silent, quietly stuffing himself with everything in reach until he was starting to resemble one of those new, fantastic balloons. But I was now too good humoured to scold him for it, and I called for another pint of claret, recharged my pipe, and announced, 'We're doing very well;

we're doing famously. And now, my horrible litttle monster, I've a mind for entertainment; so you shall sit here and tell me how you came to be a chimney sweep boy and your experiences.'

He was by no means unwilling, and I gave him a mouthful of the mulled claret and he started, 'I don't recollect my father, naturally, nor yet me mother for that matter. First I know was a begging academy kept by Mrs. Bagot. There was five of us, and it was very proper, we had to wash our faces every day, and we had a most weeping story writ out by a screever that we'd lost our mother and father in a cruel fire and we was left to the poor widow of a clergyman, suffering herself something wicked with the rheumatiz, so we was on the streets to beg an honest copper to help the poor soul on her way. Done very well with it too, only Mrs. Bagot always reckoned I'd got a fleery grin on me face as made all but the most simple guess that we was gammoning, specially when they started asking questions, and she used to beat me black and blue to make me look sorrowful; and more than ever when she was in the gin. So in the end she sold me to Mr. William Makepeace, the Practical Chimney Sweeper, for a crown piece. Well then...'

But I was not to hear the end of this edifying tale, at least not this time, for who should come in then but Backus carrying another folded paper and saying, somewhat more impressed than with the last one, 'There's a fellow here from Hartingfield; all of a lather. He says to give you this, sent by her ladyship.'

Wondering what now I opened it out; and it said, 'Mr. Sturrick at the Kgs Hd; in haste. Sir; I require your immediate attendance. Matters has come to light in the last hour which put me in fear of my life; also touching the death of the late Ld. Hartingfield. I send this by a good man who will bring you here most surely. Louise-Marie; Lady Hartingfield.'

VI

I read the note through again, considering it, for I was too old a duck to be brought down by this kind of shot. But it was in a woman's hand sure enough and, from what I had seen of my lady, in her manner. Apart from that there was no more to be read, study it as you might, and I commanded, 'Send the man in.' In fact he was close behind Backus and appeared on the instant; a big fellow of the servant sort though he looked honest enough, for what that was worth in this village full of rascals, and I asked, 'What's your name?'

'Nicholas Trott, your honour,' he answered.

I recollected that the coachman Buckle had spoken of a first groom by that name, but said, 'I didn't see you this morning.'

'No, your honour. I was at my work in the stables, it not being my place to enter the house unless fetched.'

'And how did you come by this?'

'Mrs. Gotobed sent for me, your honour, and brought me up the back stairs to ladyship's parlour. And ladyship give me the paper and says "Trott, you're to take this without fail to Mr. Sturrock at the King's Head. Ride fast and go secret by the back of the house and across the heath, for I want nobody to know of it."'

I considered the man again, by the look of him as simple as an ox, and asked, 'How were the ladies when you left them? What was their manner?'

That foxed him somewhat, and he scratched his

had. 'Dunno as I'm much judge. Mrs. Gotobed in a tizzy, but ladyship were pale, you might say. Asking your pardon, she said we was to haste.'

'We'll haste fast enough,' I told him, 'when I give the word,' and turned to Backus. 'D'you know this man?'

'I've seen him about,' Backus answered. 'He works at Hartingfield right enough, if that's what you mean.'

There comes an occasion when every Bow Street man has to reckon with some such chance as this, and it's not made any easier by baulking. Half a dozen times before now some poor fool has tried to get himself clear by waylaying me, that being these people's manner of thinking, and so far I've always come off the better. Moreover, nobody shall call me chicken livered; and also there was a chance that this might lead me on to something fresh. I made up my mind without more delay and said to Backus, 'Have my boy put his horses in the chaise.'

'Asking pardon, your honour,' Trott cut in, 'Ladyship said we was to go secret in case there's them about the Hall watching for us. Nor you won't get a post chaise the back ways across the heath, and I've brought an arse for you. It's not all that far; and not snowing now, though dark.'

Still somewhat suspicious I called Maggsy to me and went up to my chamber, where I got into my top coat and capes and looked to my pistols to make sure they hadn't been tampered with. The boy watched me with a plain anticipation of blood and I said, 'Now, I shall hold back this fellow as long as I can and you're to roust out the post boy and have him get a horse and follow; and another fellow with him if he can find one. We're bound to go up the lane to the heath and then bear off to the left.'

'D'you reckon somebody's out to cut your throat?' the wicked little creature asked. 'I'd like to see that, I would. But I'd be happier if you paid me that sixpence you promised afore you go.'

There was no answer to this except a smack across the head, which I gave him, and then repaired to the yard. Trott was waiting for me with two hacks, but there was nobody else about, and I said, 'I hope that beast's quiet.' I've a fair seat but I don't enjoy the exercise and I don't trust the brutes; they're bigger than I am and have a way of thinking that don't chime with mine.

'Bless you, sir,' he answered, 'as quiet as a suckling child and sweeter tempered. Up you goes,' and then, as I hitched on my pistol holsters, he asked sharpish, 'What's them?'

'Barkers,' I answered. 'Well primed and light on the trigger.'

'Begod,' he muttered, 'I hope we have none of that play, for I'm an honest man.'

'If you are,' I replied, 'you're one of the few about this damnation village that is. Now keep a steady pace; we'll get there sooner that way than doing a gallop and coming arse over tip.'

Without saying any more he led the way up the little hill, past the cottages and out on to the corner of the heath, with my horse following his quiet enough. It was a dark night and not snowing for the present, though enough on the ground to see by; a clump of great black elm trees, a bank of thicket like the mouth of a pit and an old leaning signpost with but one arm to it like a gibbet. I kept my ears pricked but there was never a sound except a pair of owls screeching at each other and another answering the melancholious creatures, the jingle of our bridles, the crunch of hooves in the snow and, once when we passed through a little dip, the crackle of skin ice under it. Nor no sound of that rascally post boy who should by now have been following behind. True enough he might say it was none of his business, yet it would have paid him to make it so if he was nice about getting his money; but he was most likely as drunk as as fiddler's drab in the taproom.

This heath was a gruesome place. Not above spitting distance of the village, but never a light to be seen anywhere. We passed through another thicket, with me watching for any sign of movement and that fellow leading as if he was steering his way from this tree to the next, under a squat old oak with one great limb sticking across as it were all ready for a hanging, and out into a dim glade with a coppice at the far side and hemmed in all round with dark scrub. I was just about to call out to the fellow asking was he leading us deeper into the forest when he started to sing; not loud, only just above a breath, but clear enough for me to catch once again that wicked, canting doggerel.

'*The sun may shine through a London fog, the river
    run quite clear,
The ocean's brine be turned to wine
Or I forget my beer,
Or I forget my beer, my lads,
Or the landlord's quarter day,
Before I forget my own true love
Ten thousand miles away.*'

I believe to this present day that the villain breaking into song then, and me knowing that vile transportation catch, was a special warning sent to preserve my life by Divine Providence. Without it young Maggsy would not be setting down this tale for your pleasure and instruction now, with me cuffing his head time and again when he makes a mistake. But here is a moral observation for you; that although the Almighty may see fit to send a warning to the righteous He still expects them to have their own armament ready. So letting fall the rein and gripping the hack with my knees as best I could, I drew both pistols from their holsters and cocked them; and at the same time, as if he had heard the double click, the rogue in front clapped heels to his beast and was off.

I was in a dilemma. Prudence demanded that I should turn about and get back the way we had come. Yet to do so was to present my rear to whatever villains were waiting; and how was I to do it having no control of my horse? Moreover the pestiferous animal, seeing its stable mate away like that, lets out a wicked snort and bolts after it; I was damned near unseated and before taking breath to get out above one curse we was in the trees. On the instant a dark figure rose up on the right while another one reached at the bridle; and without more ado I discharged my first pistol, to be rewarded by a hearty scream. One of 'em went down for certain.

But then that damnation horse, never being under fire before, give another scream to wake the dead, rose on its hind legs and bolted in right earnest. I fancy somebody got kicked, because I heard the blow and yet another cry, but had no chance to reflect on it because I was flying through the sky myself with never a moment to utter a prayer. I landed with a bump that felt like it had pushed my arse up through my shoulder blades,

103

and my second pistol blew off with the shock. But I was near enough lost, for there was more of the villains yet; and being waiting for some time they could see me better than I could them. One of 'em was over me swinging a cudgel before I could draw breath.

Nonetheless I resolved to sell myself dear. Regretting only that the thing was shot or I would have castrated the villain with an explosion, I thrust my pistol into his lower belly in a ferocity which gave the wretch pause. Yet another was on me then, also with a stick and this time it came down a crash on my beaver; it was only that trusty hat, still miraculously upon my head for I habitually plant it firm, which saved me from a fatal mischief. Even so it was crushed about my ears and I was rendered dazed, though not before I had planted home another shrewd blow. One of them kicked at me, mouthing vulgar abuse, and him I tossed over; but though still grappling valiantly, not without some return injury for what they was inflicting upon me, I gave myself up for lost. Yet you shall note that Divine Providence is ever at hand to succour the worthy so long as they attend Sunday Service from time to time; and as He had sent the warning so He did not desert me now, for as in a dream I heard the thump of horses' hooves, voices shouting, the crack of a whip and another scream.

As in a dream I saw a horse ride down the villains, damned near trampling on me too, and heard Maggsy screeching lewd curses at them; then they broke and ran. It was a vastly unbecoming posture for a man of my importance, lying on his back like a poor beetle, so somehow I thrust myself to my feet clutching my beaver and crying, 'After them; after the rogues.' But they were already crashing through the thicket some distance off and the post boy reined in and turned back, while Maggsy fell to pounding the snow off me, still screeching and capering. I said testily, 'Have done, you little imp. Be after them.'

Answering, 'Not likely; they'm on their own muck heap, and there's reason in everything,' the post boy swung himself down. 'You're a fine gamecock, by God, a roaring soldier and you've winged one of 'em for certain. All the same we'm having you back to the Head; you owe me money and I'll not see you murdered till I get it.'

'There's blood everywhere,' piped Maggsy.

'You can follow 'em tomorrow,' the post boy urged, 'you can follow that blood like a hound in good daylight. But let's get out of this now. These horrible trees all round give me the creeps.'

Cursing the fellow I examined the blood. Sure enough there was a good mess of it leading off very plain along the track; it would lie for days so long as it didn't snow again, and even if it did there was bound to be dogs to hand. To tell the truth I was of no mood for further conclusions, still having a particular sore arse, so they found my pistols while I repaired my beaver as best I could, and then got me up upon the horse, sitting very careful. Thus we made our way off that fatal heath, Maggsy galloping alongside in a manner that made me wish to have my cane at hand, and the post boy leading the animal and chuckling and laughing; being three parts drunk, the rogue. It was a sorry cavalcade but not without honour, for I had acquitted myself very properly against no less than four of the rogues. Nor was I without gratitude to the post boy and, though blenching at the cost of it, I told him he might take a pint of hot rum toddy at my account.

Saying little to Backus except that I'd taken a toss from my damned savage wild horse, I repaired to the parlour, calling for a pot of mulled claret for myself and the same of ale for Maggsy. There I had the fire piled up with fresh logs and settled to rest and reflect; while Maggsy, contenting himself only with saying, 'This is the life, this is; I'd like it fine, if only you'd give me that sixpence,' fell silent too for a wonder.

In spite of our adventure being very near the end of me I was not displeased. I now had a very fair solution to the highway robbery – as indeed you might have yourself by now since I have set everything down most scrupulously for you to consider – but still did not know which one to choose of the four naughty people most likely to have murdered my Lord Hartingfield. Or whether, in fact, there was not some sign of another as yet unthought of.

I had just about resolved that whether Sir Tobias liked it or not tomorrow must be another day of questions, together with certain other stratagems, when Master Maggsy felt that he had now been quiet for too long and piped up, 'I reckon my lady done for his lordship. She being a Frenchy and Frenchy women well known to be fit for anything; they used to sit with their knitting and watch their king get his head knocked off. I'd like to a seen that.'

A remark so wanting in respect to majesty spoiled my composure and I said sharply, 'You're a wicked little monster. Get out of my sight. But see that the fires's nice and bright in my chamber before you settle yourself. And on your way have Mistress Bet attend on me instantly; and tell her she's to bring quills, paper and ink.' The evil little imp grinned at me, plainly

106

suspecting another rollick, and I roared, 'Be about it; while you've still got a head on your shoulders to take with you.'

So I sat waiting until at last I began to fancy that the over-bold wench was going to dare me and I should have to fetch her myself; I cannot put up with unbiddable woman and I was just starting out in a fury when at last she appeared, high flushed and defiant. She was carrying the writing gear and she slapped it down on the table saying, 'I've but to shout and Uncle Backus'll come running; and half a dozen more with him.'

'There'll be no need,' I told her, not altogether disliking the spirit in her eyes and the set of her lips.

She was near enough some other sharp reply but could not escape from her feminine nature and curiosity and said instead, 'Your post boy's saying that you was set about by a gang of footpads on the heath and near beat to death if he hadn't come up to save you.'

'That be damned for a tale,' I answered. 'I put the rogues to flight myself. I'm not so easy done for.'

'Aye,' she snapped, 'and that's a pity too.'

One must ever be patient with the young, and I controlled my rage by an effort. 'Come now, girl, you're not helping yourself. Nor Godsave neither. Did my boy tell you he's likely to be charged with murder?'

'A wicked, blood-thirsty villain that boy is,' she announced. 'But I blacked his eye for him.'

'And no doubt he deserved it. I asked a question, girl.'

She tossed her head as pert as a jay. 'There's them who're better than you will save Tom when needs be.'

I nodded at her, smiling softly and saying, 'Thank you, me dear. You've told me all I want to know. They'll save him all right, if they're not in trouble

107

themselves; which is very likely.' She looked a bit fearful then, or as fearful as that Bouncing Bet ever could, and I added, 'But let it pass for now. There's another matter. Can you write?'

'I went to the dame's school.'

'But not had much practice since? Well, you shall try, Bet. Take a paper and quill and set down what I tell you.' She gazed at me wondering what I was at now, but she took up a quill innocently and I said, 'I'll go slow and easy, one word at a time. As follows; "Given by me, Bet Backus, to Mr. Jeremy Sturrock at the King's Head. I declare that Thomas Godsave could not have had any part in the killing and murder of my Lord Hartingfield..."' She did pretty well so far, forming the letters carefully with her tongue stuck out, but she stopped there and gazed at me, poor silly bitch. 'Write on now,' I encouraged her, 'you're doing very well. "The killing and murder of my Lord Hartingfield because to my knowledge on that night he was at..."'.'

Upon this she flung the quill away and pushed herself up, crying, 'I'll not; it's a trick!' She hammered her fists on the table, screaming at me in good earnest, the vixen. 'I'll not do that on Tom.'

'You'll give yourself the vapours in a minute,' I observed, and added, 'Well enough,' affecting to be resigned. 'I see you've got me beaten. Be off with you then.' That silenced her, and she stared at me uncertainly before turning away to the door. But I stopped her, calling, 'Mistress Bet.' She looked back at me over her shoulder and I said, 'If Master Maggsy is ever lewd and indecent with you again, black his other eye.'

So, chuckling, I turned to compare the few words writ by Bouncing Bet with the summons supposed to have come from my Lady Hartingfield; and it was certain the girl had not written that. For one handwriting was firm, though by no means graceful, while Bet's was the hand of a child and set askew on the page. Moreover where my lady, supposedly, had inscribed 'Mr. Sturrick at the Kgs Hd' Bet had put 'Mr. Sturuk at the King's hed', and so on. I will confess that I was glad of it, having no wish to see the silly bold bitch deeper in trouble than she was now, though it was much what I had expected. But you must note again in the matter of detecting that when you set about what we call the elimination of suspects you shall take account of all of them, even the most unlikely; and it was certain that had she a mind, as she certainly had the wit, Bet could have set up that little trap with the help of Backus. Fortunate for her she had not.

So reflecting that the time might yet come when the wench would name her first pup after me out of gratitude and that I'd sooner drink at a christening than a hanging, I turned to other matters; an epistle of my own and in my most genteel style. Bet had spoiled the quill with her heavy hand and I sharpened it daintily first, having a pride in my calligraphy, and then wrote as follows. 'Sir Tobias Westleigh at Westleigh House. Sir; prsnting my compliments, this to inform you that this night about two hrs since I received a summons from my Lady Hartingfield to attend her immdtly. This she sent by a fellow, one Nicholas Trott, who brought with him a horse for my convenience. Perceiving the matter to be of some import I set off on the instant.

'We had not prcded more than half a mile or so upon the heath, however, when we were set on by a gang or covey of villains. Upon this the fellow who should have guided me bolted incontinently and I was left to hold the field alone. Discharging the first of my armament I struck one of the rogues in some portion of the anatomy as yet unknown while my mettlesome steed kicked down another. But then by some mischance being unseated myself two more of the miscreants fell upon me. After a short but bloody affray they likewise was put to flight and my postboy and clerk arriving about then we were left the victors. By now the assailants had made good their escape carrying the wounded with them, but in view of the dischargement of my pistols, the darkness and the uncertainties of the heath, it was concluded not to follow them for this present.

'Nvrthelss a fair mess of blood was left behind and a considerable trail across the snow. Seeing this and the villainous nature of the attack I thrfre now request that as J. of the P. for this Parish you will provide me such men as are suitable, who shall be armed with fowling pieces or muskets and pistols or the like, together with dogs which can sniff out the trail if it will presently be covered with fresh snow. Thus we shall bring these miscreants to immdte Justice. I propose to attend upon Her Ladyship the early part of the forenoon, as you receive this, to propound certain questions to the persons of her household with an end to the speedy termination of this business. Thereafter I shall wait for you at Hartingfield, if you desire to be present in person, or if you have other occasions will lead the hunt myself.

'With respct, Sir, I subscribe myself your mst obdt servant, Jeremy Sturrock, at the King's Head.'

A very fair letter I considered, and I read it through again with some satisfaction, stowed it in a safe pocket and took myself to bed. Maggsy was snoring like a little hog upon the health and for an instant I was tempted to take out a silver sixpence and lay it by him, but thought better of it and busied myself about recharging and priming my pistols instead; that being a consideration which no officer of the law should neglect, together with his prayers, when retiring for the night.

I arose refreshed, stirring up the child with my foot to have him go down and tell them to prepare my breakfast; and by scarcely an hour more we were setting out again in the post chaise. For a wonder the post boy was in a high good humour, evidently of a mind at last that I was a most admirable client, Maggsy as bouncy as ever, and a bright, pretty day; even that pestilential heath, with the snow sparkling and the trees looking less wicked than ordinary beneath a blue sky, was such as to arouse poetical observations in my breast. But I had weightier matters in mind and I first gave Maggsy particular instructions; chiefly that once I was in conference with the other servants he was to seek out a certain ancient cleaning woman of the Gotobeds and engage her in conversation about her work in the house, especially on the morning after the death of my lord. Then, on arriving at Hartingfield I produced my letter to Sir Tobias and directed the post boy to deliver it to Westleigh House and thereafter take himself off to the stable yard there, where he was to keep his eyes and ears keen in every direction.

Gotobed opened the door, somewhat whey faced at seeing me again, and I noted he made no remark that I should have been here last night. I said, 'To wait upon her ladyship.'

'At this hour?' he asked, looking as if he was about to weep. 'My lady will scarce be risen yet.'

'The matter brooks no delay,' I told him. 'Acquaint her of my presence.'

There's no arguing with me when I use that tone and he went off, most certainly to find Mrs. Gotobed, while I was left to cool my heels. It would have suited me then to visit the wine cellar; but I judged it impractical, and waited patiently until at last the woman Gotobed appeared, with the expression of her own face somewhat resembling a chamber pot had it been less bony.

She led me up to the little parlour, where my lady was still reclining in the same blue mantle trimmed with white fur. No doubt a pretty and elegant figure of a young woman and perhaps more than sweet with Sir Tobias, but again she gave no welcome and did not ask me to be seated, her manner being that I was something between a servant and a low person coming to collect a debt, as in a way I was did she but know; nor did she say anything of me being called here last night either. Nevertheless I put my best knee forward and bowed at my most genteel, saying, 'Your pardon for the intrusion, my lady; but there are certain matters I must take up with you.'

She seemed indifferent, though keeping her eyes veiled. 'Indeed? But Gotobed is attending to the formalities. I'd a thought you could deal with him.'

'Not so, ma'am,' I answered. 'I require your personal assistance. And, in a manner of speaking, you instructions.'

Raising her eyebrows she considered me coolly out of the arrogant hazel eyes, a provoking smile on her lips. 'Sir Tobias,' she said, 'opines that you are a pompous bullfrog of a man.'

'Does he, my lady?' I asked, restraining my choler. 'Then Sir Tobias should know. He is a gentleman of excellent judgement.'

'A bullfrog of a man, and not to be taken too much notice of,' she continued.

'As to that, ma'am, and with respect, he is in some error. But I should consider it unmannerly to dispute on the matter.' I gave her another bow, clinging tight to my gentility and asking, 'May I have your attention and assistance, my lady?'

'Why not?' she replied. 'It'll be a divertisement in this damned dreadful desert. What is it you want?'

'You have a pretty, elegant writing desk and quills and paper all ready,' I said. 'Will you be so kind as to seat yourself there, my lady, and write as I shall dictate?'

Even she could be taken aback it seemed for she stared at me in astonishment, saying, 'Write you what? A billet-doux? Lord, what a mysterious bullfrog it is.'

I bowed again, thinking that I would have the better of her yet. 'A short notice, ma'am; and the offer of a reward.'

She looked at me as if I were a clown or pantaloon. 'A reward? For Hartingfield? God's Blood, sir, how much d'you think he was worth?' But then the set of my face must have rebuked her, for she had at least the grace to lower her eyes and shrug, and then cross over to the escritoire. 'Very well. I'll give a crown piece. It's a small round sum.'

A most shocking observation, but I told her, 'You must be the best judge of that, ma'am. And this is not the matter of my lord. We shall settle that a different

way. This is for information concerning Thomas Godsave. Also leading to the recovery of your jewels.'

'Godsave?' she repeated. 'He had no hand in this,
you know. That coachman's a rascal. You should look
for Roderick Medfield.'

'Very likely, my lady,' I agreed. 'But we must find
Godsave first. And most of all we must find your jewels.
If you permit, I'll dictate the form such a notice
should take.'

She narrowed her eyes at me but shrugged again and
took up a quill. 'Very well, if you must. Let's have
done with it.'

'With pleasure, my lady,' I said. 'As follows; "Given
to Mr. Jeremy Sturrock of the Bow Street Runners,
lodging at the King's Head in Roehampton. Wanted
on suspicion of highway robbery, one Thomas Godsave..." ' I watched her write that and continued,
'And now, if you'll be so kind, a short description of
the man.'

'Damnation,' she cried, 'everybody knows the boy.
Moreover, Mr. Bullfrog, do you imagine I spend my
time gazing at servants?'

'It may be necessary to have this posted in London,
ma'am; and in all cases it is the correct form to include
a description.'

'By all means let us have it in the correct form,' she
said and turned back to writing again. "Brownish hair
inclining to red, fresh complexion; blue eyes, good
white teeth. Not above middle height, but well
shaped." So,' she asked, 'will that do?'

'Excellently well,' I assured her, 'it's a living picture
of the fellow. Now we come to the reward. With your
permission, we continue; "For the recovery of certain
jewels stolen and purloined from my Lady Harting-

field in her coach a reward ..."' I stopped, eyeing her ladyship shrewdly. 'What d'you consider, ma'am? A nice round figure now.'

'Why,' she answered, 'I consider nothing at all. But I'll do as is customary.'

'These days,' I said, 'it is most often ten per centum of the full value of goods recovered.'

'Lord, man,' she cried, 'I'm no mathematical philosopher. What's that?'

'On thirty thousand, ma'am,' I said, 'three thousand; guineas.'

'Three thousand guineas? Three thousand fiddle-sticks. I'll give two hundred.'

'Ma'am,' I suggested, 'I fear that sum would merely be a cause for laughter. Shall we say two thousand?'

'What care I? Five hundred.'

'A highwayman can buy himself off for that. Fif-teen.'

'It's a pertinacious Mr. Bullfrog,' she mocked, vastly enjoying herself, for it is well known that these French women love to haggle. 'A thousand; a thousand guineas, and not a sou more.'

I bowed once again, recognising the time to give way. 'A thousand guineas. A neat figure and worthy of a certain interest. So we continue, "A reward of one thousand guineas will be faithfully discharged by the undersigned". And now, my lady,' I finished, more respectful than ever, 'you put your name.'

All agog with merriment, in which I was somewhat tempted to join myself but kept a straight face, she scratched "Louise-Marie, Lady Hartingfield", saying, ' 'Tis an empty gesture I fear; we shall never see my jewels again. Yet does that satisfy you?'

'But for one thing,' I answered. 'A document of such

115

weight should have a witness. An honest, upright and reputable man.'

'You'll need a lantern to find one in this house,' she said.

'Your butler?' I asked, 'Mr. Gotobed?'

She gazed at me for an instant and then broke into a veritable peal of laughter, yet not without a touch of rage behind it I thought; like that impudent footman had said yesterday, laughing her head off in her own boudoir. As a gentleman should I affected not to notice, and at length she stopped and got out, 'Lord, sir, if you fancy Gotobed's an upright reputable man you're the very simplest of all simple bullfrogs. But if that's what you want, have him in. Be pleased to ring the bell.'

While we waited she flung back to the daybed, clearly in a fine sudden rage – which I found of interest – and I studied that valuable document. I have already said it is my habit to kill several birds with the same stone, and the first of these was that it was clear she had not written the note last night; for the hand-writing was of another style and she had spelled my name different and the King's Head. I was not surprised; but you shall observe that it was another one marked off. By that time Gotobed had appeared, standing there as respectful as a mourning mute, and with a more than common edge to her voice my lady said, 'Gotobed, Mr. Sturrock requires you to witness a document.'

He bowed, and I asked, 'You can read and write?'

'Why yes, sir,' he answered, offended that I should put the question, and I nodded to the paper on the escritoire. Bowing once more he came across and took up the quill; he could not fail to see what was writ there and gave first my lady and then me a long look, but then examined the point of the quill and at last wrote down "William Gotobed, Butler", fair and square. I waited for it to dry and then folded the sheet and stowed it away in my safest pocket.

My lady's face was curiously mixed of mockery and anger, watching me and Gotobed, but she asked, 'What now?'

'Not to trouble you further, ma'am,' I said, 'but touching the late Lord Hartingfield. I would like a small closet or chamber where I may question all your household servants one by one.'

She seemed indifferent again. 'As to that you must do as you wish. 'Tis a pity to hang some poor wretch for him. He was scarce the value of a man's neck, but I imagine the law must be satisfied. See to it for Mr. Sturrock, Gotobed.'

So dismissed we bowed ourselves out; and, following Gotobed down the stairs, I was again not dissatisfied. A bullfrog Sir Tobias might consider me, but we should see who'd croak the loudest in the end; moreover a bullfrog with a thousand guineas tucked up his weskit is a damned fine bullfrog anywhere.

VII

They found me a closet, and by God's blessing a handful of fire in the hearth, with a door at each end so that the rogues could come in at one and pass out of the other without having a chance to communicate to the others what I'd asked them; a most important matter in the art of detection, this. Then being set up with paper and quills and ink I called in the first one; who turned out to be the smallest and ugliest child I ever saw barring Maggsy, like a little brown mouse and stinking near enough like one too. But, ever gentle with the lowly, I set her at her ease by saying, 'Now, me dear, there's no need to be afraid, I shan't eat you; not today. A question or two and we've done. You'll be Nance?' She jerked her head up and down, more like a mouse than ever; a mouse that couldn't have had a part in any of this business, and I contented myself by asking simply, 'Well, Nance, the night before last, gone ten o'clock, where were you?'

'Why, sir, in bed; snugged up against Poll for the warm. For she's good to me, whatever some of 'em say about her.'

'There's a sensible girl,' I said, 'and a clear answer. But before you went to bed, Nance, did you hear anything of my lord and her ladyship having words in my lord's private cabinet?'

She was at once fearful and excited. ' 'Tisn't my place. I'm never let past the green door but early in the mornings. Only Poll and Mrs. Peascod was there alistening for all they was worth. Till Mrs. Gotobed come and druv them away.'

'But they'd be sure to talk about it?'

'Talked o' nothing else,' she whispered. ' 'Twas concerning Mr. Roderick. About him having the property. And him a terrible wicked man.'

Apart from that there wasn't much more to be had from her and in the end I gave the child a ha'penny, sent her on her way in transports of delight, and had the next one in. This was Poll, and a naughty bold eyed grig she was. It didn't take much looking to see where she was bound for, and as likely from choice as need; the streets of London first and one of the three natural endings after that. But I said, 'Now, Poll, there's no doubt you've got your head set on the right way.'

'I can see what's to my advantage,' the saucy miss answered. 'And there ain't much of that in this house.'

'It's quiet, eh? But not always. What happened the other night, Poll? When you and Mrs. Peascod was listening at the door?'

'Old Lord Screw and Lady Highnose having another go.'

Reflecting that if a great many people ever knew what was said about them in their servants' halls they'd fall incontinent into the vapours, I asked, 'Another go? So it happened often?'

'Now and again. More so since she lost her jewels.'

'You're a sharp girl, Poll,' I told her, 'and likewise you've got sharp ears. What was said?'

While I considered the wench, reuecting that she'd be the better of a whipping, she recited, 'Lady screeches "Then be damned, sir, do what you will, for I want none of it" and he bawled "By God, madam, you'll have none, better Roderick than a French whore; I'll see you on the streets yet". Then it sounded like she was cussing but I couldn't make that out being an outlandish language, till she does another screech, "Twould be worth it, knowing you was dead".'

'Well,' I said, very soft. 'That's plain enough, ain't it?'

'Plain enough for anybody. She done for him.'

'Did you hear any more?'

She shook her head, the trollop. 'Madam Fart, Mrs. Gotobed that is, come then and druv us back into the kitchen.'

'I can see they don't let you have any pleasure. Where was you that night, gone ten o'clock?'

'Well abed and asleep,' she answered.

'What?' I asked, 'all alone, a pretty girl like you?'

'Don't amaze yourself, master.' She gave a giggle. 'There's never a man in this house I'd take to bed. Not for less than sixpence, and they wants their rides for nothing. Hack tried it once in the hay loft and I very near crippled him for life. I was with little Nance, poor toad. She ain't much, but she's warm.'

'And you've a good heart to go with your looks,' I said. 'So tell me, Poll. What d'you make of this Tom Godsave? Could he have done that highway robbery?'

'Tom? God help you, Tom'd never have the spirit.' She leaned forward at me across the table. 'I can tell you who done that job. Who but Master Roderick?'

You may be sure I did not like this; for if true, as it could be, it set all my own answers awry in a most damnable fashion and my plans with 'em. With somewhat more sharpness I said, 'Come girl, that's a very serious matter. What makes you say so?'

She tossed her head at me. 'He was here six months

back. Trying to borrow money off my Lord Screw, no doubt, and in a right rage of not getting it. Well then, he was romping Madam Snot ...'

'And who,' I asked, 'in your elegant speech, might that be?'

'Why, Mistress Clarees, the lady's maid. He was romping her in the hay loft, and he said he was minded to turn highwayman and how would she fancy that? That's for sure, as I heard it myself.'

'You'd seem,' I observed, 'to spend a fair part of your time in that hay loft.' She gave me a bold look in answer; and I pressed her. 'Come now, my girl, let's have it all. What else?'

Turning sulky at my tone she answered, 'He's a gay gallant, and a good horseman. And he's thick as thieves with Buckle the coachman. So if Buckle see him the other day he'd as like as not say it was somebody else. And Tom Godsave'd do. Tom's soft.'

'So where is Tom Godsave?'

'Made away with. Master Roddy wouldn't think twice about that.'

The slut was oversetting everything, but I said, 'That'll do then, except for one more thing. Can you read and write?'

There was no need of the answer, for this kind have only one accomplishment if you can call it such, and I dismissed her and sat considering for a minute or two, wondering about this tale of Captain Roderick. But I comforted myself by reflecting on Bouncing Bet's pertness and my lady's own very plain attitude. Yet it was possible for even me to be wrong, and I offered up a prayer for that thousand guineas which I had thought was as good as in my pocket before banging upon the table for the next to come in.

This was the wood boy, one Samuel Kite and a bit simple. He had heard nothing of the quarrel on account of being in the harness room with the coachman and Nicholas Trott, sitting over a brazier and listening to tales of highwaymen – and a fine beggar's opera they made of them I've no doubt – until Mr. Hack the footman came in saying that 'They was at it again', meaning lord and ladyship; and Nicholas Trott had a can of rum, which they gave him a sip and then told him to take himself off. I nodded to show approval and said, 'Now boy, you was in bed before ten, but you crept down again on the quiet and you heard somebody moving about the house.'

It near enough frightened him to death that I knew of that, but when he'd done stuttering he got out, 'I wasn't up to nothing, only starving cold and looking to lie by the kitchen fire. And Mrs. Peascod'll sometimes leave out a hunk of pie where I can find it, me being known to be always hungry.'

'That's all very fine,' I said. 'But you'd use the back stairs if you know your place. So how did you come to hear somebody in the house? Was you pilfering out there?'

'No, sir,' he cried. 'I swear I warn't. I never went out. Only somebody come to the green door, end of the servants' passage, and pushed it open a bit and stood with a candle; like listening. So I was frit to death and lay quiet.'

'Who was it?' I asked.

The poor little pig was uneasy about that, but I pressed him, and at last he blabbed out, 'Mrs. Goto-bed.'

'Did you see her?'

He shook his head. 'Heard her stays a creaking. Stays

always creaks when she breathes heavy. I got right sharp ears.'

'And did your sharp ears catch anything else?'

He appeared uncertain again. 'Kind of smash.'

It looked as if the lad was trying to fancy up something to satisfy me and I said, 'Let's be sure of this; what did you hear?'

'Kind of smash,' he repeated. 'Like when Mrs. Peascod knocks something over in the kitchen, being drunk. Dunno what it was though. 'Twasn't very much.'

'You're doing well,' I encouraged him kindly. 'When was this? Before or after you heard Mrs. Gotobed's stays creaking?'

He had to think about it, but at last he whispered, 'Before. A bit after I crept down to the kitchen. Mrs. Gotobed come to the green door about eleven; I heard the stable clock strike not long after.'

'That's very good. And was there any more?'

'I dunno,' he answered, watching me like a little owl. 'Not that I know of. I just kept still where I was.'

I considered this, thinking that if he was lying on the hearth the sound of something falling might travel through the floor where he wouldn't hear anything else, reflecting also that if I tried to press him he'd be pretty sure to over enlarge on it, and then went on, 'Now tell me this. Did anybody come through the kitchen?'

He shook his head, suddenly fearful again. 'No sir. Wasn't nobody. Mr. Buckle was boozing in the harness room with the others.'

'And Mr. Buckle,' I said, 'sometimes comes through to take a bit of what he fancies with Mrs. Peascod. Is that it?'

'Please sir,' he answered obstinately, 'I ain't a going to say no more, lest I get my throat squeezed same as his lordship, like Mr. Hack warned me.'

'Come, my lad,' I told him sternly. 'What else was there? Out with it.'

'Somebody tried the yard door,' he muttered.

'And what time was this?'

'Dunno,' he cried. 'Please, sir, leave me be; I'm fearful. It was about after I come to the kitchen; before I heard the bump.'

After that there was little more I could get out of the lad, try as I might, and I dismissed him also with a ha'penny; but reflecting that I must curb my natural extravagance and generosity, for it was getting the better of me.

Mrs. Peascod was next, a tearful woman and of shape which made it plain that Coachman Buckle liked his pleasures bountiful. From her I learned that her sorrows commonly came on her that time of night and she most often took a drop of something to comfort herself, nor did she know where Buckle was on this occasion; she went to bed well before ten. Her I disposed of in short order satisfied that she hadn't the wit for anything much above gin, and sent for Hack the footman. Still an impudent rogue I fixed him with a hard look, announcing, 'Now, Hack, there's one man already well on his way to the gallows for this business,' – which was true enough though I didn't yet know who he was. 'Have a care you don't go with him. Night before last you made the fire up at nine o'clock. Was her ladyship with my lord then?'

'Brushed past me as I was going in. Damn near knocked me down; and cursed me for it. She's the one who done for him.'

'When I need your views I'll ask for 'em,' I said. 'Where was you after that?'

'Dicing in the harness room along with Buckle and Nick Trott. Nick'd got a quart of rum and we was right merry.'

'Nick Trott,' I mused. 'That rogue's name keeps coming up. I'll have him in next, when I've done with you.'

'Begod you won't,' Hack answered. 'Nick's gone missing. Ain't been seen since last night.'

I regarded him narrowly, murmuring, 'There's no doubt about it, my man; you're well on the way to Newgate. They say the condemned cells there are such that men are thankful to be hanged to get out of 'em. So Trott's gone missing. Where to?'

Even after that awful warning the bold rogue grinned at me. 'How should I know? But he've got a doxy at the inn by the telegraph.'

'So,' I said, 'we've got a doxy at the inn. And it seems Coachman Buckle's got one here too. Was the kitchen door out to the yard and stables left undone that night?'

'No. It were locked fast.' The rogue looked more sullen and impudent than ever and added, 'Look you now, master; if you mean did one or another of us come in and scrag his lordship you're barking up the wrong tree. We was all so drunk we couldn't have throttled a kitten, let alone him.'

'What?' I asked. 'Three fine rogues like you and but a quart of rum? What are you; men or babies? Where did you get it?'

'Trott's doxy works at the inn. She nicked it for him.'

'I'll be damned,' I said. 'But I must see this Trott

myself, for he must be monstrous good on the job. The payment's commonly t'other way about.' I studied the rascal, worrying him, and then demanded, 'Can you read and write?'

He stared at me for a minute before asking, 'God's truth, what d'you think I am? A parson?'

'You look more like a poor class rogue. How d'you know the yard door to the kitchen was locked?'

The fellow eyed me cunningly, but then answered, 'Trott. We thought to get a bite to eat, and Nick Trott went to try for it.'

'So that's the way of it,' I said. 'Very well then; you can be off. But don't kick your heels too high or you might find 'em dangling instead.'

I had Coachman Buckle in next, a man of very different sort from Master Hack, and to him I presented an amiable manner as one good sportsman with another. First I went through the business of could he read and write – to which he answered that he could, claiming to be a pretty fair scholar – and then tricked him again into setting down a statement to Mr. Jeremy Sturrock at the King's Head. This went off as I expected, proving that neither had he penned that naughty little trap last night. But I was not disappointed, for you shall note that by now I was becoming nicely curious to sort out most of all which of them could read in this household; and bearing in mind the letter or document my lord was writing about the time he was murdered you shall note also that so far we have only her ladyship, Mr. Gotobed and Buckle; with Mrs. Gotobed yet to come.

That being done and still very amiable I turned to the questions, asking, 'This Captain Roderick, Mr. Buckle. Did you ever hear that he was minded to set up as a highwayman?'

He gave a laugh. 'I wouldn't be surprised. For he cares neither for God, man nor devil. And a damned fine horseman.'

'Yet you're sure my lady's highwayman was Thomas Godsave?'

'I am,' he answered shortly. 'That I'll swear to.'

Thinking of my thousand guineas I was vastly relieved, yet there was still one point troubling me and I said, 'I'll tell you what I don't understand. If Tom Godsave had planned to purloin my lady's jewels why did he let himself get recognised? Wouldn't he have tried some disguise or concealment?'

'He did,' Buckle averred stoutly. 'Wearing a cloak and this bag over his head. Twas his bad luck I was too smart for 'n. And I wouldn't a knowed but for holding the pistol in his left hand, as I told you. Likewise the little finger of the other was cut off at the stump, him being nipped by a filly sometime while trying to look at her teeth.'

Satisfied now, I observed, 'I always said horses was savage beasts. Now, Mr. Buckle; you, Hack and Nicholas Trott was all together the night my lord was killed. Until what time would that be? And did any of you leave the harness room? Mind you,' I added, 'we're satisfied that Godsave's our man, but I like to have everything clear.'

'As to the first,' he said, 'me and Hack was there till well gone twelve. And for the other we all went out at one time or another; to relieve ourselves.'

'That's natural enough. And which of you tried the kitchen door?' He did not answer that, but there was the look on his face which I had noted yesterday. I asked, 'Nicholas Trott? I'll tell you what I think, Mr.

Buckle. I think by that time you was all a bit tired of rum and Trott said he'd try to find you something different. And,' I added, 'it goes on at all the great houses, and where's the harm?' thinking at the same time that if many of 'em were such fine fornicating places as this one God help the landed gentry.

I winked at him, and so encouraged he fell into the trap, 'I won't say but Nick has his own way of getting round old Gotobed.'

'That's what I thought. And I wish he was here now, for I'd like to have a word with him. But maybe you can tell me, Mr. Buckle. Does he read and write?'

Buckle shook his head. 'Never a word; he's no scholar, Nick. Though he says Sir Toby reckons it'd pay him to learn at least a little bit, so's to look after his own interests when the need arises.'

'Sir Tobias?' I demanded, perhaps somewhat over sharply. 'What's his interest in Nicholas Trott?'

Surprised by my tone the man stared at me. 'Why, but Sir Toby's training him to be a pugilist; a boxer.'

'So ho,' I said, 'so that's the fellow Sir Toby's interested in. And don't they fight practice bouts at the inn by the telegraph?' I was so taken by that as to sit contemplating it for a minute or two, before I finished, 'I'm obliged to you, Mr. Buckle; I'm most particular obliged. And I'll not keep you any longer.'

I sat for above another minute reflecting curiously on this and then called for Mrs. Gotobed, who came still wearing the expression of a chamber pot a size too small and half filled with vinegar; and somewhat cold with outrage that I should dare to call her to witness along with the lower sort. There's none so rare of their dignity as these upper servants; I've seen 'em in the royal households and you'd think they was majesty itself. Though in no mood for such fancies now I still put on my second best gentility. But the first thing I asked took her fair and square between wind and water. I said, 'Ma'am, it's an extreme of kindness to attend me when you've so much on your hands. So I'll be short with you. Can you tell me how this household will stand if Captain Roderick Medfield takes the property along with the title?'

It was quite true, what the boy said, that her stays creaked; begod she could have taken a part for an obligato at Covent Garden. Moreover she pursed her lips, looking by now like a chamber pot with a spout to it, – which is a thing I never saw though no doubt we shall have them soon with all the new inventions in this rude and critical age – and finally got out, 'I was not aware that any such disposition is likely. Nor, to be plain with you sir, that it's any business of yours.'

'Very plain,' I murmured. 'A short answer, simply put and most proper. So we'll come to the happenings of that night. As I understand Mr. Gotobed went into my lord's cabinet a little after ten. So he was the last to see my lord alive.' You must note that I had not meant anything particular by that question, but it seemed to me that she caught a little breath on it; not much but enough to make me think there was something here worth pressing. 'The last to see my lord alive,' I repeated. She still did not answer and I rallied her, 'Come ma'am, is there any doubt about it? If there is it might well be important.'

'Not the last alone,' she said finally. 'I was called in to his lordship myself. He . . . He wished to make some complaint about Mrs. Peascod.'

'Mr. Gotobed was present? And that's all the matter?'

She lowered her head, which I took to be a nod, and I continued, 'So his lordship, then still living, was most likely seated at his desk and just about or just finished writing something. Did you see what it was?'

'I do not look over my lord's shoulder at his business.'

'Quite so. That not being your place. But not a quick take in? Would it be a letter; or a longish document? Maybe entering up his daily journal, as so many of the peerage keep.'

'I did not see.'

I remarked to myself again that all the women concerned in this matter were as stubborn as donkeys, but said, 'Well now that's a pity, for it leaves us with something we don't know. But let it pass. You was about in the hall again, gone eleven o'clock.'

This time the stays let out a creak like a veritable trumpet blast. She started, 'How do . . . ?' but then checked herself and answered, 'We was late up. My lord had asked me to prepare some particular accounts for the morning. It may be that is what he was writing himself.'

'Ah,' I said soft, but comfortable, 'so there we have it. There's little left now, ma'am; but I have here a paper writ by my lady.' This was lying ready on the table and I held it across to her. 'Will you be good enough to read that and say whether it's a fair and true description of Thomas Godsave?'

It was quiet while she read it; pretty quick and easy, I noted. Then she nodded, saying, 'It is some likeness of him.'

'We're doing famously, ma'am.' I said. So then I had her write a statement like the others to Mr. Jeremy Sturrock, lodging at the King's Head, watching her as she wrote, listening to the quill squeaking in the quietness. At length with a cold manner she asked, 'Is that as you require?' I drew back the paper towards me. But I did not need to more than glance at it, for there was no likeness either in the writing or spelling to that fatal note last night. Yet I was not displeased since it was clear enough now which way all things were pointing – as no doubt you will have seen for yourself – and I answered, 'You've been more than kind, ma'am, and I'll not detain you longer. Now a minute or two with Mr. Gotobed himself and we're done.'

'I'll bring him to you,' she announced.

'No,' I said, very gentle and still smiling. 'No, ma'am. You shall not trouble yourself.'

She looked wickedness at me, her stays creaking another opera, and I added, 'Allow me, ma'am, if you please,' and led her firmly to the second door. One or two of the others was still whispering in the passage beyond, but they broke with a skitter as she appeared; I closed it behind her, went back to the other and opened that, saying, 'Well now, Mr. Gotobed; I ask your pardon for keeping you so long,' and brought the man in.

I let him sit for a minute or so more while I considered. Though I wanted to have this over before Sir Tobias came storming in, as he was bound to do before long, it is often a good play to let your witness cook for a while; and, moreover, I was now beginning to perceive a certain light in the darkness. I concluded it was time to let fly a shot at random and said, 'I'll not trouble you more with this paper of my lady's, Mr. Gotobed. But I daresay it won't be the only document you've witnessed this last several days?'

You could have counted to a hundred before he answered, and then with a stutter. 'What document, sir? I don't understand. What has Mrs. Gotobed told you?'

'Why Mr. Gotobed,' I asked, 'what should she have told me? A little light, genteel conversation, no more. Let it pass, we've more important business. To come back to his lordship; you entered his cabinet gone ten and he was writing at his desk? So we've got that clear. But then he desired you to fetch Mrs. Gotobed?'

It was another shot gone home, for he gaped at me again. 'Why yes, sir, that is so. I should have told you perhaps. But it escaped my memory. Is it of much matter?'

'Very little; only to have things straight. So my lord wished to make some complaint about the girl, Poll? Is that correct?'

Gotobed fairly leapt at it. 'It is indeed, sir. A bold, indecent slut; but Mrs. Gotobed and me have been unwilling to turn her away, as if we do there's no doubt where she'll end.'

'No doubt at all,' I agreed. 'Your niceness does you credit. Where was her ladyship about this time?'

'She had retired, sir. That night her ladyship retired early.'

'And very likely,' I observed, 'seeing she was somewhat at odds with my lord. But let that pass too; nobody could fancy that my lady would do such an ungenteel thing as throttle her own husband.' The fellow patently turned a shade paler, becoming a somewhat greenish hue, and I continued, 'Now you and Mrs. Gotobed were about latish on; gone eleven o'clock.'

For the first time he showed spirit. 'I'll not be so

baited. Why should we not? We were at our lawful duties.'

'Why, Mr. Gotobed,' I asked, 'who said they'd be unlawful? I'm asking only what you was doing.'

'As to that, sir,' he answered, clearly thinking as fast as he could, 'Mrs. Gotobed was writing letters to several ladies begging one or another to find a place for the girl. We had some discussion whether we should try again to intercede with his lordship for her, but it was then near enough half after eleven and we concluded to leave it for the next day.'

And, I thought, Hartingfield most likely lying dead by then. But I had all I wanted out of this pitiable fellow now; he could scarcely keep his fingers from twitching, gazing at me as if I already had a rope about his neck, and I said, 'Lord, Mr. Gotobed, you've nothing to fear. When we have Tom Godsave you'll be safe enough. And by the look of it now you're about to receive a visitor. You'd best go to welcome him.'

For chancing to glance out of the window I perceived a most warlike cavalcade approaching. First of all Sir Tobias riding a rangy brute of a hunter with pistol holsters at the saddle, then two other fellows mounted on hacks. Behind them two more on foot, one carrying a fowling piece in the crook of his arm and the other with a pair of dogs on leash; and bringing up the rear my chaise with the post boy wearing a grin on his face as wide as London Bridge.

VIII

Scarcely a minute after Sir Tobias came roaring in, fixing me with his hard look and saying, 'So you're here, sir, are you?' thrusting the letter I had writ him into my face and demanding, 'God's Teeth what's this? Do I understand you pretend that my lady set some kind of ambush for you? My lady, you damned oaf?'

'Sir,' I said at my genteelest, 'pray moderate your manner.'

'My God,' he answered, 'I'll moderate you,' flinging my letter upon the table, and adding, 'You outrun your powers, my man; and your welcome.'

'My welcome perhaps, sir,' I rejoined, 'though I grieve for that. My powers, no.'

'Then what in hell's damnation does this mean?' he barked. 'And what's this about Trott?'

He looked likely to use the riding crop and with one eye on it, as I should have disliked laying violent hands on a Baronet of the County even to protect myself, I told him, 'Simple enough. You have the gist of it there. And here is the note sent to me last night.' That I laid before him, and while he scanned it with his brows knotted like a sailor's rope, I continued, 'I'm now satisfied it was not penned in this house. I'd say it was done by some whore, doxy or mistress of the man, Nicholas Trott. And at his instruction.'

'By God,' he swore, 'if Trott's rutting again I'll have

done with him. I told him to contain himself while in training.'

'That's your business, Sir Tobias; mine's to find him. And them as put him up to this.' I looked back at him as hard as he was looking at me, wondering if he knew how clear it was that his interest in Nicholas Trott brought him close in to this affair himself. But he did not say anything, and I finished, 'I propose to set about it this instant.'

'Very well,' he answered sharply. 'I'll pay quick respects to my lady and then we'll be off.'

While he was gone I gathered up my papers, not forgetting my own letter that he did not seem to want and which I could use for my memoirs, and passed out into the hall; where Gotobed was waiting with my hat and cane and capes fairly trembling to be rid of me. Outside it was still a bright day with quite a touch of warmth in the sun, but the snow lying crisp and pretty underfoot. Sir Tobias's fellows touched their foreheads to me politely as I passed, no doubt recognising my weighty manner, and just as civil I raised my cane to them, making for my post boy waiting at the chaise. He had a cunning, conspiratorial look about him but little enough to tell when I asked.

'It's a fine, spruce place,' he said, 'makes this one seem like a knacker's yard; and no shortage of money. Some good flesh there. Damned fine hunters and three or four hacks.' He nodded to the fellows waiting on their own horses and the other holding Sir Tobias's. 'A pony and cart for the housekeeper and four carriage hosses. Dunno as I ever see a better stables.'

'But you got nothing?'

'Naught but a pretty fair hint to mind my own business.'

135

'There'd scarce have been that if there was nothing to hide,' I said. 'Was it manner or words?'

'Manner more like. And I wouldn't make much on it. All of these gentry stables're the same; they're class and they know it. And a powerful fancy with this lot that the sun shines out of Sir Toby's arse.' The rogue grinned at me in an ugly sly way. 'Likewise they've heard all about you, guv'nor, and it seems they don't reckon a lot on thief takers.'

'Damnation to your impudence,' I told him. 'Be ready to set off when Sir Tobias comes out. You'll put me down near as you can to where we had that little matter last night, then make your way in no great hurry to the telegraph and wait.'

Maggsy appeared then, jaunting round from the stable yard, stopping to gaze at Sir Tobias's beast, and only coming on when I called out to move himself. 'God's Truth,' he announced, 'you've set 'em all by the whiskers. Ma Peascod's in screaming fits that you'll hang the lot of 'em before you've done, and old Goto-bed told me to get out of it or he'd call one of the grooms to kick me out.'

'No doubt on account of your endearing manners,' I answered, bundling him into the chaise. 'Did you find the ancient woman?'

'Easy,' the little monster boasted. 'Sitting on a stool in the scullery, nursing a cut finger and cussing her head off. So I let on I used to be apprentice to a surgeon.'

'You're too smart by half,' I told him. 'Come to it will you?'

'Had to make up to her, didn't I? I heard the lot about her rheums and belly-aches; a right apothecary's pisspot that one is. Anyway, the morning after my lord

136

got himself throttled she was set to washing the passage by the wine cellar though it wasn't the day for it, and she reckoned that made it bad luck 'cause she cut her finger on a bit of broken glass. Likewise she reckoned Gotobed got drunk the night before and dropped a bottle of port, there being a stain on the flagstones and this bit of glass.'

So here was a little more light. And you must note that this had come only from my own quickness in perceiving a certain manner about Mrs. Gotobed yesterday; a thought that in observing the old woman washing that passage I was witnessing something which held a secret.

'Is that another sixpence owing to me?' Maggsy asked eagerly.

Fortunately on that instant Sir Tobias himself came out, advancing towards us in no great hurry. He turned a damned hard look on me as if there was much he would like to say, but thought better of it, then nodded to the groom and swung up onto his horse. So we set off in cavalcade, my post chaise leading, Sir Tobias riding alongside with his hunter gleaming like chestnut satin, behind us the two mounted grooms and finally the fellows with the dogs; a most imposing sight and one to bring home to any villains who observed us that the law is not to be trifled with. It was not long before we came to the heath, and here I alighted while young Maggsy leaped down beside me in a great scutter of snow, making Sir Tobias's beast sidle and rear. One of the men very civilly offered me his mount, but I had a mind to contemplate the beauties of nature on foot, as they were very pretty all around us and such an opportunity for moral and improving study should never be missed;

137

and besides the brute had an evil look in its eye.

We passed the great elms and down through the little hollow where I remembered the ice crackling and at last came to the thicket. Here the kindly snow during the night had smoothed away the marks of our bloody affray, but I recognised the place well enough and the dogs at once set about scratching and whining, throwing up on the instant flurries of pinkish brown coloured snow. 'Seek, Jasper,' their handler called, 'Find him, Jewel,' and they set off eagerly, while Sir Tobias cried, 'Gone away,' and I waved them on with my cane. It was a fine and gallant sight.

Thus we plunged through the thicket, even on this bright day a dark and close grown place with the bushes meeting above our heads, and out onto a bare moorland rising a hill. Without fault the dogs led across it and down towards a grove of trees, all black and white and of strangely twisted trunks, and then again into another ride still more sombre and melancholy than the thicket. Here there were clear traces of blood, for being sheltered the snow had not fallen so heavy, and we pressed on faster with the dogs giving tongue and ourselves following very near at a trot. From this we came out into a clearing dotted with sparse scrub oak and fallen trees; and at the far side an old hovel or bothy built of branches and thatched roughly with heather.

Now yelping with excitement, as if they knew they were at their journey's end, the dogs made straight to it and set about scratching and whining at the rough door. We also approached, and Sir Tobias dismounted, taking his pistols from their holsters while I myself called, 'Hallo there; come out of it.' But there was no answer from the hovel and it fell curiously silent in the clearing. We waited for a full minute but there was never a sound, save one of the dogs whining softly, until I started forward, demanding again, 'Come out of it I say.' But still there was no answer, and this time Sir Tobias thrust with his foot against the door, holding his pistols at the ready while one of his fellows stood with the fowling piece levelled. The door burst back with a crash and even now there was nothing, save a pair of rats which streaked out and at which the dogs set up yelling, a wild shrill sound in the quietness. Then Sir Tobias and myself pressed in together with Maggsy, not to be outdone, close behind us. 'Begod,' the little ghoul chattered, 'the rats've been at him a'ready.'

So our man, or one of 'em, had escaped us; and in no kindly way, poor devil. He lay on a rough pallet of heather and sacking, the dead eyes staring at us and glinting in the light from the doorway, one hand trailing on the earth floor. Somebody had tried a rough surgery on him, for a topcoat was thrown across the lower part of his body and he was stripped down to his shirt, where there was a wad of bloody rag on his chest; and elsewhere yet more inhuman wounds. Even the rats of Roehampton were savages. I am not of a weak stomach and have seen many an ugly sight in my day, but he was a sad mess of mortality lying there in the gloom with the bright sunshine and the sparkling white of the snow outside.

I was contemplating some moral observation on it when Sir Tobias broke in, 'That'll be your man? God's Teeth, sir, don't look so whey faced. He'd ha' done for you if you hadn't winged him first; and better die like that than on a plank with a mob of yokels licking their chaps and waiting for the drop.' The others had crowded in and he asked, 'Do any of you know him?'

'He'm from the tinkers' camp,' one of them answered. 'Known as Windy Jack; and so called on account of he was a prodigious breaker of wind. Used to do it for a side show at fairs and boxing matches and the like. That's him, Sir Toby,' the fellow concluded, 'and I reckon her's farted his last trump this time.'

Sir Tobias nodded. 'He'll have been near enough dead before they got him so far. We'd best get him safe while there's enough of him left for Coroner Nokes to pontificise over. Begod, that bumble fly'll have a field day.'

So, instructing two of the men to procure a hurdle from the nearest farm and then to convey the mortal remains there and tethering the dog Jasper to the doorpost to keep the rats at bay, we passed out again into the sunshine. Where Master Maggsy must needs announce, 'God's Truth, this is the right stuff, this is; I wisht I could tell Mr. William Makepeace, the Practical Chimney Sweep, I bet he never see...' Him I stopped with the flat of my hand, though Sir Toby took it upon himself to laugh; which I considered somewhat amiss, for you cannot instil a proper gentility in children if their betters encourage them to the vulgar.

However we had sterner business on hand and on Sir Tobias saying, 'Leave Jewel with us, Ned; we'll see if she can pick up the scent,' we set the remaining dog to work. But the man answered, 'I misdoubt it, Sir Toby, as it'll be cold by now; they was following the blood so far, bless their clever little noses.' And sure enough the sagacious creature was beaten, though making several casts around, and showing her willingness. 'So there's no good of that,' Sir Tobias observed.

'Well, sir, what shall it be?' he asked. 'The fellow was a tinker and that would indicate their camp. Or do you have other plans?'

'The tinkers by all means,' I said. 'But we'll stop at the inn first. I've hopes we'll flush your pugilist and his woman there. Your Nicholas Trott. And I want to know who set him on to this last night.'

He gave me one of his hard looks but answered, 'As you will; one's on the way to the other. So let's get on before the horses catch a chill. But you'd best take a mount, it's a fair step from here. George, give Mr. Sturrock yours.' Seeing my face he cried, 'God, you Londoners lose the use of your backsides; she's amiable enough and George'll hold you on if needs be.'

It was an unkind cut, and I thought with pleasure of the several surprises I had in store for Sir Tobias yet; though I confess that I could not help but like the man however much against my better judgement. So we set off, but not without a certain trepidation and fear of some rude country trick such as these fellows are known to delight in; or of young Maggsy, who was trotting alongside, letting out a sudden screech and bolting the animal. However we arrived safely to find the post chaise waiting, and all dismounted. Once more Sir Tobias looked as if there was much he would like to say to me, but not before the servants, and we turned to the door.

It was a very different air from yesterday. There was no singing that damned canting song; a dozen or so hang dog rogues here again, glum but ugly, that peg leg gut scraper plucking idly at the strings of his fiddle and the landlord leaning against the counter as if in conference with them. He stopped as we entered, Sir Tobias following me and the groom and Maggsy behind, looked up nonplussed for the instant, but then put on a smile and cried out, 'Why, Sir Toby, here's a pleasure to see you again, it's long since we had the kindness!' None of us answered and he cast a sidelong squint at me, adding, 'If it's the trouble yesterday, your honour, there wasn't no harm meant. The lads was out for a bit of fun and the gentleman himself picked a quarrel.'

'That's a bleedin' lie,' shrilled Maggsy. 'The fiddler there took a snatch at my balls and ...'

I slapped my cane down on the counter, making the landlord flinch away, and roared, 'Have done. And you keep quiet, Maggsy, or I'll take the skin off your back. Now,' I said, very soft, 'you did well yesterday, my man, scouring the heath for Godsave and letting me know. It shows you've got a nice feeling for your own neck. But you can do better yet. I want one Nicholas Trott and his woman. Where are they?'

He shot a glance at Sir Tobias, clearly asking whether he should speak or keep silent, and Sir Tobias answered, 'You'd best talk, Lumkin. For Mr. Sturrock is a devil with the art and science of detection.'

I gave him but one look and continued to the landlord, 'That frolic yesterday was devilment and I'm prepared to let it pass as such. But last night there was a try at planned murder. Planned by somebody afraid that I was getting too close on his heels. And planned in this house. So if you know what's good for you you'll answer my questions. Now then; was Trott and his woman observed to be writing anything here yesterday? A note or letter?'

The other rogues was silent, watching the landlord; and Sir Tobias cut in again, 'You'd best speak up, Lumkin.'

'I'd a thought Trott was your interest,' he muttered,

but then added, 'Be damned to it. Him and the woman was scribing something over against the fire there; laughing and giggling about it.'

'What then?' I demanded.

'Then Trott says "Does anybody here fancy to try conclusions with that robin redbreast at the King's Head?" And I told him I'd have none of it, I'd had enough trouble from you and didn't want no more. So he answered "If that's the way you feel we'll try them as have guts in their bellies instead of wind". And that's the truth,' Lumkin finished, slapping his hand on the counter. 'That I'll swear to.'

The others muttered and grumbled something between themselves and I observed, 'I hope it is for your sakes. Right then; this woman. Who is she? Would her name be Clarice d'Arbois?'

He gazed at me dumbfounded and then said, 'I never heard of her. This one's Meg Budd. Used to be a governess over Richmond way but got turned off on account of being too quick to lift her knees behind her ears. So she took to screeving and whoring.'

'And I will say,' I announced, 'that never have I seen such a damnation fornicating place as this Roehampton. If I'm about here much longer I shall be afraid for my own virtue. Screeving,' I explained to Sir Tobias, 'Is the trade of writing begging epistles and conning letters; mostly for rogues. So where are they now?' I asked the landlord. 'This pair of daisies?'

'Not here,' he muttered. 'Not since early morning. They both took out then. I gave 'em shelter on account of the snow. God's Truth, Sir Toby,' he burst out, 'I didn't know what they'd been up to.'

'Though you might've made a damned good guess,' I told him. 'Where are they?'

'Tinkers' camp,' he confessed at last. 'They was planning to set off for Guildford after dark tonight.'

'So ho,' I said. 'Then the tinkers' camp it is.' But there was still one more question, for though I was by now pretty well certain of the part Captain Roderick played in this I like to see everything covered; and, moreover, it would not do any harm to have Sir Tobias fancy I was still hunting on the wrong scent. I asked, 'How long since was Captain Roderick Medfield last seen about here?'

That surprised the landlord, but he answered readily enough. 'Close on six months. And I'm sure of that for if the captain'd been around he'd have showed himself. He likes a drink in good company.'

'And welcome to it,' I rejoined, turning to lead the way out again; not without perceiving a certain twist of amusement on Sir Tobias's lips. There we reassembled our cavalcade, and I enquired, 'Now then, can I get my post chaise up to this encampment?'

'Near enough, sir,' the groom, George, replied. 'But wishing your pardon, you'll do best to think twice.'

'What troubles you, George?' Sir Tobias asked.

'You know as well as I do, Sir Toby. They're little better than cannibal savages and there's ten or twelve of 'em, to say nothing of the drabs. And never a one but ain't wanted for something or another and the way they look at it is that you can't hang twice. They'd cut your liver out for a pastime.'

That I knew could well be true enough. There are places in the stews and rookeries, as there are certain flash houses – notably the Brown Bear – where they may know who you are, understand that you're the law and what they'll get for their handiwork, and yet still set out to kill you for the merriment of it. The rogues always reckon they have a chance to escape; and the damnation of it is that they often do. But I had questions to ask and an account to settle. 'For God's sake,' I demanded, 'Shall four free born Englishmen be set at defiance by a rabble of ruffians?'

'I'm a warning you, that's all,' the fellow insisted doggedly. 'You'll have trouble.'

'Come George,' Sir Tobias told him, though not without a laugh at me, 'are you going to let a Londoner outface you?'

'Leave the thief taker to try his own conclusions, Sir Toby, that's all I say,' he argued, these damned countrymen being as obstinate as their women. 'If you goes, we come with you, that's for certain. I'm only saying what to expect. But if I was you I'd send one of us the short way across the heath, to make sure none of that lot in there don't ride over fast to warn 'em as we're coming and to be ready for us.'

'Now,' cried Sir Tobias, 'that's a sound notion. I'll go myself, for Chestnut needs warming up and Jewel can come for the run. You and Jem there will escort Mr. Sturrock. Let's be away,' he finished, 'and we'll see some sport yet,' swinging up onto the hunter and cantering off round the outbuildings of the inn, whistling to the dog.

After some colloquy between the two grooms and the post boy we started off; and, as might be expected, little of that exchange had been lost on Master Maggsy. He seemed to be torn between his natural and most horrible propensity for blood and mischief and a certain fearfulness; observing, 'Mr. William Makepeace, the Practical Chimney Sweep, always used to say that if you was going to get mixed up in a mill to make sure you was going to get t'other rogue's tripes before he got yours. Otherwise not to stick your nose in where your arse couldn't follow.'

'Doubtless,' I answered, 'a very proper sentiment for a villain. But I've a job of work to do.'

'No,' he said earnestly, 'but this life suits me fine. Riding about like a lord, a belly full of vittles all the time – I never thought anybody could ever have his belly as full as I've got mine – and the promise of sixpence; if I get it. But I don't reckon I never shall,' he continued. 'You being the gamesome cock you are you're sure to be in the thick of it; Mr. William Makepeace, the Practical Chimney Sweep, was a flea-bite to you once you get started, a most awful quarrel-some man you are. All the same everybody knows what tinkers is too; and if they gets your guts for skipping ropes, which is most likely, what happens to me? First thing I shan't never get that sixpence; and second I shall be cast off again, and I'm spoiled for chimney sweeping now.'

The little rascal entertained me and I answered kindly, 'When Providence stretches out His Hand to you, boy, He very rarely draws It back.'

'Ain't so sure of that neither,' he sighed. 'Seems to me He's always faster to stretch out His Big Boot than His Hand; can't never tell when He's a waiting ready to poke another one up your breech.'

'What, you cantankerous rascal?' I cried. 'You blas-phemous lump of stinking soot, would you dare to argue divine theology with me? Be silent, you goose witted little ape.'

By this time we were approaching a yet wilder part of the heath, a mysterious and gloomy copse to one side, and on the other a wasted upland with a single riven tree black against the snow; over the rise of the hill another dark bank of forestry, and above that a thread of smoke rising into the sky. Here our two grooms turned off the road, for what little that was worth, waving us on to follow them over what must have been a damnation rough track under its soft deceitful covering. So lurching and jolting we went on at little more than a foot pace for a time until the post boy stopped, shouted something at the grooms and turned back to me. 'Journey's end, guv'nor,' he announced. 'Go further on this and if we don't lame a hoss we'll break a spring, or if we don't do neither we'll go tail over tip.'

It was a waste of breath to dispute with the surly rogue, and indeed there was no time to. For even as we drew up there came the bang of a pistol; not above half a mile away by the loudness of it and from somewhere beyond the nearer stand of trees. On the instant we stopped as if set into ice ourselves, gazing that way, before one of the grooms said, 'It'll be Sir Toby.' Hard upon that came another explosion, and with one man still listening the other looked round to me saying, 'Master, if that's Sir Toby in trouble we'm bound to go to him.'

'Be damned to that,' I said. 'You're at my orders.'

'Asking your pardon,' he answered, and before I could get another word in they both touched their horses and went off at a gallop, crashing into the wood with snow flying at their heels.

So we were left with our force down to two men and a boy; and one of them uncertain, since the post boy would doubtless say it was no affair of his. But without speaking, my face set in its hardest mould, I descended from the chaise, laying my cane upon the seat and taking down my pistols. 'Begod,' he cried, 'you ain't a going it alone?'

'What else?' I asked. 'I've work to do.'

'Now listen,' he begged. 'You heard what was said. This lot'll fillet you as soon as look. And don't you see that Sir Toby might've fired them two shots to call his men off and leave you to it?'

I did indeed; nor had it escaped my notice how our power had been reduced on every excuse since we set out. Chance that might have been; but equally so it was not unlikely that Sir Tobias had made the most of it, and was now away about his own arrangements leaving me engaged here. But even the best of us, even Jeremy Sturrock, can only follow one line at a time; and I am not a man easily put off. I said nothing, merely looking to the priming of my pistols, while Maggsy shrilled, 'You won't turn him; he'm a terrible man. And I'm a going anyway to see the fun.'

I started up the slope, hearing the post boy cursing behind me, saying, 'I wisht to God you'd pay me what you owe and I was well out of this.' But I went on without answering and he bawled, 'Least I'll turn the chaise. You damned fool; you might want to get away fast, or be carried away.'

'Mr. William Makepeace, the Practical Chimney Sweep, wouldn't a done this,' Maggsy chattered. 'He were a very cunning man was Mr. Makepeace.' Only in time did I recollect that I was holding a pistol in either hand, for if I had struck him with one of them I should have done the devil a mischief and, what was worse, lost one of my two precious shots.

The trees was not so thick as they had looked and beyond them was another clearing; a dirty, sluttish place, as these people make everywhere they go. There was a round topped wagon and another with a canvas hood, a big tent and two smaller, and three or four unkempt horses; one black old hag crouching over a fire and cooking pot, and a drab with dugs as big as oatmeal sacks giving suck to a brat. Over against the bigger tent there was a black bearded rogue tinkering with a copper kettle and sitting by one of the wagons was a second, whittling at a piece of wood with a long knife. We ourselves stopped in the trees – for the post boy had caught up with us now, puffing a bit on account of all the ale he drank, but carrying his whip – and surveyed this disgusting scene, while I said, 'You two keep here so long as all seems peaceful. If it looks like turning rough you may come out and do what you can. Not that it will. These fellows don't like pistol balls.'

'Neither does gamecocks like knives, mister,' the post boy grumbled, but by that time I was already stepping out. The one sitting at the wagon watched me coming for a few paces and then got up himself, still holding the knife, and approached me just as slow. None of the others moved or spoke, except the old witch at the fire let out a cackle and squeaked, 'Here's a pretty gentleman come to dinner.' So we came up together step by step until the villain said, 'What d'you want of us poor folk, your honour?' His canting voice belied his damned ugly looks.

'No harm to anybody here,' I told him, 'but for one Nicholas Trott and the woman, Meg Budd. Them I mean to have.'

'If that's the way of it,' he whined, 'take 'em and welcome. They're nothing to us. But who might you be?'

'Jeremy Sturrock,' I told him, sharpish. 'The Bow Street Runners. And here in discharge of the law.' But I observed that he had changed his hold on the knife, now having it with his thumb and finger pointing along the blade, which you shall note in your own protection is the grip for that most wicked and vicious lower belly thrust. I said, 'Drop that knife or I'll shoot it down.'

'Well then, shoot away,' he answered. 'We don't fret ourselves about the law. That's for the gentry, master; it don't mean much to wandering people. You'll be the one as shot poor Jack?'

'And you too, you rogue,' I cried, 'if you don't keep civil;' for the temptation to attack the whining villain and be damned to it was already growing on me.

'No, but you wouldn't.' He shook his head, showing his broken teeth in a dog's grin. 'There's others as'd shoot you. We knowed you was bound to come. You're a violent and terrible man; and 'twas a wicked business killing poor harmless Jack.'

And, by God, they were waiting for me. The fellow with the kettle was now nursing an ancient blunderbuss, a most horrible and maiming weapon at short range if it don't burst itself when discharged; there was another in one of the wagons with a fowling piece, and one more stepping out from behind it with a pistol as good as my own aimed over the crook of his arm. Not to mention two or three others and Nicholas Trott and an overbold flaunting bitch that I took to be his woman.

Behind me in the trees the post boy chattered, 'For Sweet Jesus' sake come out of it, they'll gut you,' but I held my ground. The play was to keep 'em talking and make no retreat, for they was like mongrel dogs again, vicious but chary of taking the first bite though once they started there'd be murder done. I said, 'And a wicked business to leave poor Jack to die in that bothy.'

'They couldn't do naught else, your honour. Was another lad cruelly kicked by your arse and they couldn't manage both on 'em. And Jack were already gone.'

'So you shouldn't try conclusions with me. And fools to try them now. Come out, Nicholas Trott,' I called. 'I'm taking you for questioning and the woman Meg Budd for uttering a forgery of my Lady Hartingfield's signature.'

That trollop had the impudence to laugh at me, and the whining rogue answered, 'Why if you want 'em you can have 'em. But why don't we see a bit of sport for it? Nick's a notable man with his fists; if you beats him you can take him. So honour'll be satisfied.'

There was no doubt what the dogs intended, but little else I could do. Not for His Majesty himself would I have turned and walked off that field, and for sure got a charge of shot in my back on the way; moreover a bad chance is better than a worse certainty and I thought I might give Master Trott a surprise or two. 'If that's the way you fancy it,' I said. 'But a fair, straight contest. And we'll see who comes off the better.'

IX

I called my support out of the trees, for what it was worth; the one clinging to his whip as it were the last hope but the other grinning like a jackass at the prospect of his favourite and horrible pleasures; mischief and blood. Nevertheless he whispered, 'You'll flay him, master; but I wisht you'd give me my sixpence first.' Turning a reproving look on the little monster I handed my pistols to the post boy, though the tinker rascal cried, 'No, your honour; lay 'em on the ground.'

'That be damned,' I answered. 'You'll have it my way or none at all.' Watching 'em close I affected to be careless of the other rogues, preparing myself for the battle at leisure and dignity as a gentleman pugilist should. Stripping off my capes and coat I handed these with my beaver to Maggsy, settled my neckcloth more daintily and drew on my gloves again, for I am habitually nice about my hands; in my shirt sleeves the air struck chill but I reflected that in a minute or two no doubt all would be warm enough. 'Have a mind to what you owe me,' the post boy whispered urgently, 'and fight your way back into the trees so's we can run for it,' while one of the villains jeered, 'Ain't in no hurry, be her?' and I answered, 'All in good time, my man.'

They was closing round in a circle now, above a dozen of them; or more with their dirty sluttish women, and all too near for my liking. With my long experience of weighing the chances and making my plans I had already decided that the best tactic was to fight in close, so that they with armament dare not fire for fear of killing their own man. But I still wanted room for it and none of the treacherous scum too tight on my back, and I cried, 'Stand off there. If you want to see sport give us room for it.' They should have no cause to fancy that Jeremy Sturrock was afraid of 'em.

Even as I spoke there was a crackling of hooves in the trees and Sir Tobias and the two grooms rode out; a damned fine rescue brigade, only a shade too late. They reined in sharp and he cried out, 'God's Teeth, what's this?' though it should have been plain enough for him to see. I fancy also that the fellow with the fowling piece must have levelled it against him, as he roared, 'Lower that thing, my man, or I'll see you flogged for it.' But looking to Sir Tobias, the instant of inattention, was near enough my undoing; for Trott rushed at me of a sudden and caught me a smart blow on the neck and almost before I could put up my defence landed another to my jaw. It was a rascally trick and I was forced to give ground, while the ugly pack around us howled their joy.

Better than half a stone heavier than me he had a longer reach and, as I quickly perceived, was pretty well trained. This was to be a bloody business and I resolved to let the rogue fancy that he was toying with me, putting in a smack or two as I could until such time as he grew over confident and careless, when I would punish him for it. I got in a glancing tickle at his jaw, a mere nothing, and then seemed to open my defence upon which he let fly a terrible swing at my head. This I avoided by ducking sideways and under,

153

but then planted a shrewd right hander on his nose and followed it at once not by a left hand swing, as he might have expected, but by a second right jab to the mouth; it is a quick move if you have the science to do it, and remarkably disconcerting. He stepped back, spitting and cursing in surprise while I rapped an upper cut to his chin and heard Maggsy screech at the top of his voice and Sir Tobias cry, 'Well struck, sir; excellently well struck.' It was a particular pleasure that Sir Toby seemed to be enjoying himself.

However I was not to have it all my own way for Trott caught me a pile driver which half jolted my head off and, warding aside another, it felt as if my left forearm was broke. Knowing that once struck down I was done for, with or without Sir Toby's kindly interest, I gave ground to gain time to recover, fooling my opponent into thinking that I was near enough done. But when he came after me for the kill I feinted with my left at his nose, let him put up his guard, and returned the like pile driving compliment with my right in the pit of his belly; following this by a round arm slam at his left side just below the ribs. That steadied the rogue, but little more than winded him, and we went on at it hammer and tongs, too busy even to hear the screeching and hullabaloo all round us.

It was still anybody's fight though he was puffing a bit now, and I let on again to be weakening myself, taking punishment but contenting myself warding off the most of his blows. He was a poor simple fool and that brought him to over confidence again; to teach him manners I got in a left feint at his lower ribs once more, and the instant he brought down his guard put in a right to the nose which must have damned near flattened that organ against the back of his skull.

Dazed by this and expecting another from my left he put his hands up, whereupon I gave him two wicked ones, right and left to each side of his belly, following these with a round chop to the kidneys. That was about the end of it. Whooping for breath he leaned forward and, being a man as likes to make sure of the matter and no nonsense about being over tender, I planted another on his nose and a swinging right with all my strength behind it at the angle of his chin. It more than paid for any I'd taken, and if his jaw wasn't broke it said much for the strength of his bones.

He went down like a felled ox; and the noise of the others, which for some minutes had been alarm and consternation, swelled up to rage. In an instant they was on me, even that black old beldam with all her claws out. Her I thrust off with the flat of my foot and she went smack on her arse in the fire, where she lay battling with the cooking pot and hooting like the bagpipes till somebody dragged her out of it with her clouts singeing. But I had little time to observe such niceties for we were fighting for our lives. The fowling piece went off and I still swear I heard the shot whistle past my ear; there was the crash of a heavier discharge, the scream of a horse, the snarling of the dog Jewel, and Sir Toby roaring curses. While this was about that whining villain came at me with his knife, but I was in no good mood for genteel exchanges now and I twisted at the rogue's wrist, breaking it I fancy, before taking him by the gullet and casting him also on to the fire; a very proper place for him.

I caught sight of Sir Toby's fearsome chestnut red hunter rearing and squealing and lashing with its forefeet, while the grooms danced their mounts and laid about them like cavalrymen. Then there was a shot from one of my own pistols by the sound of it, the post boy yelling, 'Whoa back there you rats,' and Maggsy, the merry little rogue, snatching a brand from what was left of the fire and making to set one of the drab's skirts ablaze; but being foiled of that by her kicks running to do the same office for the tent, as in the meantime the dog Jewel worried at the buttocks of another wretch. But I was got busy again, for one more of them rushed at me with a cudgel or the stock end of the fowling piece, catching me a glancing blow which laid me down; nevertheless I took his knees as I fell and the two of us rolled pummelling each other over the supine body of Nicholas Trott. I was forced to half throttle the fellow to be rid of him; the which I attended to with zest being somewhat out of patience by now. But on getting up again I spied Trott's woman, Meg Budd, making off across the heath and I bawled to the grooms, 'After that bitch; I want her alive,' so despatching them in pursuit.

But peace must descend at last even on the most fearful war. We were left to survey the stricken field, and a pretty sight it was. The old hag sitting with her naked breech in a patch of snow, doubtless to cool the fiery smart, and the other with her clouts up about her hams beating out the smoulder, while behind her the tent blazed merrily. That rascal with the blunderbuss sitting against the wagon wheel as black as Maggsy's Practical Chimney Sweep with his weapon split from end to end – a fault you should note they're liable to if you overload them with old nails and such, which is a common mistake. Another crouching and nursing his shoulder with blood trickling down it, and a satisfied but astonished look on the post boy's face which betokened that he'd fired the shot; two that had been struck down by Sir Toby's hunter or the grooms, three others lying along with Nicholas Trott that I'd accounted for alone, and one making off with Maggsy hallooing and hurling stones after him. 'So ho,' I murmured with some satisfaction, turning across to Sir Tobias, who with the other groom, was examining a light scare or wheal across the chestnut's flank.

He turned an eye on me near as wicked as the horse's, for these gentlemen are as nice about their animals as they are of human flesh. 'By God, sir,' he observed, 'you're a bellicose gamecock; and a damned fine pandemonium you set up. Couldn't you have waited?'

'Gamecock yourself, sir,' I retorted roundly. 'Or rather slow cock. For I'd made sure you'd left us to it.'

'To hell with your impudence,' said he. 'What kind of man d'you take me for? I spied two fellows coming from the telegraph, put one shot across their noses to warn them off, another behind to speed 'em on their way, and took after them myself. Chestnut needed a canter, she was cold.' He gave one of his laughs. 'But I'll forgive you, for that was a rare good mill. Trott had you outclassed yet you used your head the better. But mind you'll have to watch those low punches of yours; some of 'em came close to being damnation dirty. And what now, with this lot?'

'I'll seek to mend my ways, sir,' I answered. 'As to this I've got the two I want; for the rest it's your juris-diction. I'd say they've had a sharp enough lesson and can be left to lick their wounds.'

'And this pair?' he asked, for one of his men was dragging Trott to his feet and the other approaching with the wench, leaning from his horse with his hand in her hair and laughing at her curses; a bold eyed grig, not unhandsome and for all her low Roehampton language plainly a cut above the company she'd been keeping.

'I'll need some place to question 'em,' I said, and added with a certain cunning, 'your own house'd be the best. And examined in your presence as Justice of the Peace.'

It was plain he did not care for that; but neither could he escape from the duties of his office, and he answered shortly, 'Very well then. My fellows shall bring them to Westleigh and we'll meet you there directly.'

Leaving Sir Tobias to ride off the field with the two grooms driving Trott and the woman after him, we returned to the post chaise much after the manner of the conquering heroes; both the post boy and Maggsy vying with the other as to which had done most fatal damage. The post boy claimed it was his extravagant marksmanship with my pistol which had proved the decisive stroke, but Maggsy argued in his delicate way that had it not been for him and Sir Toby the rascal with the knife would have had my guts around my knees on the instant after I downed Nicholas Trott. But I let them talk, since it is ever the manner of the lower sort to celebrate another's victory, only demanding silence when we were once in the chaise; for I needed time to reflect, consider, and in short to devise another stratagem.

You will by now have perceived how matters stood. I knew who had stolen the jewels and why; likewise who had murdered my Lord Hartingfield. I knew what that document he had been writing was, and what significance it had in this whole affair. So why not finish it and have done? you will ask. There are two very simple answers to this. The first being that at the inquest tomorrow I wished to present our booming barrel of a coroner with something so clear that even he could get it into his thick skull; and the second that I must needs look to my own interest. To do so much would need a nice diplomacy and perhaps even a certain light bending of the law; but in this I was persuaded that it would right a sad wrong, and you will recollect moreover that in my early years I served a period as an attorney's clerk. Turning all this over in my mind I at length conceived a plan which gave me some pleasure; a piece of dramatics perhaps, but as this business had started with play acting so should it finish, and thus achieve a sweet artistic roundness.

By this time we were approaching Westleigh; a very fair house of brick in the more modern style with some fine stands of timber in the park, which could be seen even under the snow to have been set out in the prevailing fashion of landscape. His Majesty, who has an informed taste in such matters, would have considered it a most comfortable commodious residence and I could do no less. My reception was equally genteel, being met by an elderly and most respectable and courteous butler who took my capes and beaver and conducted me to Sir Tobias's study; a light elegant room again after the fashion, but mannish enough, with none of your French fripperies about it. Three or four good armchairs where a man might take his ease and smoke a pipe, a few shelves of books to show that he was of a philosophical turn when he had the mind for it, a pair of pictures of horses by Mr. Stubbs, and a desk well covered with papers.

Sir Tobias himself was standing against the fire with

his foot on the fender, unbuttoned and with a glass in his hand, but plainly the master here. 'You made good time, Mr. Sturrock,' he greeted me. 'A glass of madeira?'

'Twould go down very grateful, sir,' I answered.

He nodded and turned to pour it, and then continued, 'You'll permit me to observe that tricking my lady into signing a warrant of a thousand guineas reward for her jewels was slim; too damned slim by half, Mr. Sturrock. And I suppose you think you'll be handling it?'

'Your health, sir,' I answered, taking the glass from him. 'The warrant does not specify any names.'

'It appears this art and science of detection is a formidable matter,' he mused, returning to the fire, standing with his foot on the fender again and gazing down at the burning logs. 'That thousand guineas, sir. You'll never touch it for you'll not find the jewels; they're lost by now. What would you reply if I was to say that you'd do best to go back to London and own yourself beaten?'

'Why, sir, the simplest answer. That I'm not. Permit me to observe this is an uncommonly fine Solera. And now with your permission I propose we have the man Trott and his woman in.' He gazed at me once more for a long instant before ringing the bell, and I added, 'I'll ask you to allow me to conduct the examination however strange it may seem. And since we must above all frighten this pair will you be good enough to seat yourself behind your desk like the very figure of justice?'

They came in with the grooms behind them, Trott being in a sorry state; I was surprised myself to see how many beauty patches I'd landed on the poor fool's face. But the woman was still brazen and defiant and plainly the one to take down first. I said, 'Now, Meg Budd, you are in the presence of one of His Majesty's Justices of the Peace; and I am about to lay an information against you to the effect that you did feloniously utter and forge my Lady Hartingfield's signature with intent to cause harm to me, Jeremy Sturrock, as an officer of the Law. The penalty for that could be hanging or at least transportation to Botany Bay for life; and you may be certain that Sir Tobias here will commit you to trial.'

She told me what I might do with myself in a manner which I shall not set down here for fear of offence, and I was deeply shocked to observe that Sir Tobias very nearly laughed at her. But restraining my choler and pursuing my own plan I continued, 'Which of these it shall be, and perhaps a flogging into the bargain, or whether I persuade Sir Tobias that it was a mere mischievous prank and beg him to let you go free depends upon Nicholas Trott here. You I have no interest in; if whoring were a capital crime the half of London'd be empty in a twelvemonth. Therefore if he tells the truth there's nothing against you. D'you understand that, Trott?'

'Well enough,' he answered. 'Meg had no part of it anyways. Only to write what I told her to put down. And thinking it were no worse'n a toss in the snow for you.'

'Just another rude Roehampton pastime,' I commented. 'Still you do yourself no harm to be honest. So your job was to lead me into it, singing that thieves kitchen ditty for a signal, and then make yourself scarce. But who put you up to it, Nicholas?' He did not speak, and I fancied that Sir Tobias was waiting on him more than I; for I knew the answer. 'Come now,' I said, 'let's not be bashful. I'll tell you myself. The Gotobeds.'

That surprised him, as indeed it would have surprised me in his place. He was too dim witted to see that it must be false, but just bright enough to perceive that it might advantage him. 'Aye,' he muttered at last. 'I dunno how you guessed; but that's right.'

'No,' Sir Tobias burst out. 'It's damned nonsense.'

Shooting him a warning look I continued, 'And what was the payment to be? A bottle of port?' Again Trott did not answer, but this time looked both fearful and cunning with it. 'A bottle of port,' I pressed. 'That being a pretty regular thing.'

He said, 'They Gotobeds'd been feathering their nest out of his lordship for years, a bit at a time. Me and Buckle knowed about it and there was many a favour they'd do us to keep our traps shut.'

'That's what I thought. Now then; let's go back to the fatal night when my lord was murdered. You, Buckle and Hack was dicing in the harness room over a quart of rum. But you yourself went out alone about half gone ten. What for?'

'Why,' he answered, brightening up. 'What for but to piss?'

'Begod,' I observed, 'you must've had an uncommon full bladder or a stricture to be so long about it in that weather.' You will note I did not say how long, for I did not know myself; but that frightened him once more and I went on, 'No, my man; I'll tell you again what happened. By that time you'd got tired of the rum and you said you'd try for something better. So you set out to the kitchen door but found it locked, Mrs. Peascod not being in a mood for Buckle that night. Being drunk and somewhat obstinate you then went on to the Gotobeds' private entrance. Was that fast too?'

The fellow was turning a yellowish hue under his natural colour and the bruises I'd presented him with and I demanded, 'Why so sickly? What's a bottle of port, man? It don't interest me; I just want to know whether that door was locked too, so Thomas Godsave couldn't have got in that way.'

Sir Tobias seemed about to cut in again; but Trott licked his lips, looked mightily relieved of a sudden, and got out, 'Aye; it was. But the parlour window were lighted and I scratched on that.'

'So now we see it clear,' I said. 'Gotobed came to let you in, you did your business with him and he most likely put up a bit of an argument as he was bound to do. And while you was about it Thomas Godsave broke in at the front of the house and quietly throttled his lordship with nobody any the wiser. Purest chance, my man,' I concluded. 'And only Godsave to blame for it.'

'No,' Sir Tobias exploded once more. 'I say it's nonsense.'

Fortunately on that instant the woman Budd let off also. 'God rot you,' she screeched, 'what's this of mine, and how long am I to be kept here?' adding several observations which I shall not soil this pure paper with.

'Not a minute longer,' I answered. 'Sir Tobias, no doubt you've a village lock up? So let her be taken to it and held there until tomorrow after the inquest. Then we'll decide whether to let her go free or not; with or without a whipping.'

With what I considered an unseemly levity Sir

Tobias nodded to the grooms and they turned to lead her away. I shall lower a discreet veil over what followed save to remark that never would I have thought one of the gentler sex capable of such fancies; such observations on the most surprising peculiarities of our persons, our abilities as men, and other matters. Sir Tobias's fellows seemed to be enjoying the affray, as did our sporting Justice of the Peace, while at one point Trott declared that he'd not see Meg so handled until I reminded him pretty sharply where he stood himself.

But at length the woman was removed, peace restored, and Sir Tobias remarked, 'A spirited wench. But you're a fool to mount that sort of filly, Nicholas. You'll finish with a dose of pox and that'll be the end of any hope in the prize ring for you.'

'And that's where I'd most like to see him,' I said warmly. 'For I love a good, bold fighter who can take his punishment. But now let's get back to business. They tell me that you can't read nor write, Nicholas. Is that true?'

'Never a word of either,' the poor idiot answered, now a lot more cheerful than he'd any right to be.

I nodded, and then affected to be in some doubt, seating myself in one of the armchairs and gazing abstractedly at Trott, saying nothing until Sir Tobias asked, 'Well, sir; what now?'

'That's the devil of it,' I confessed. 'I'm not sure myself. It all hangs on some paper or document my lord was writing a bit before he died. You'll note there's only four people in the house who could have understood what that was and what it meant by reason of being able to read. The Gotobeds. Buckle – but I'm satisfied he's out of it otherwise he'd have answered

certain of my questions different. And her ladyship.'
Sir Tobias stiffened, giving me the hardest of his looks
yet and I added quickly, 'Her ladyship's unthinkable.
So that leaves the Gotobeds.' I seemed to forget Trott
standing at the corner of the desk and mused on,
'There's no doubt they took that paper. And that they
knew my lord was dead by some time after Trott left.
But how to get 'em to admit it?'

'Perhaps by your art and science of detection,' Sir
Tobias observed.

'Well no, sir,' I answered mildly. 'The art and
science of detection's done its work by now. What I
want is a confession; and I shall use Nicholas Trott to
get it. That's it,' I told him. 'I shall have you tell your
whole story at the inquest tomorrow; the business of
your bottle of port and how the Gotobeds set you on to
lay that ambush for me. They'll talk fast enough then;
the more surely when I lay certain matters of my own
before the court.'

I will confess that to me, and perhaps to you also,
this was as full of holes as a collander; but Trott was
too simple to see them and even our Sir Tobias was
almost as nearly taken in. Nevertheless Trott turned a
shade towards yellow again and cried, 'No, your honour; I'll not do it.'

'You'll hang if you don't,' I told him. 'You and Meg
Budd. I've quite enough against both of you if I choose
to use it. And if it's a matter of necks I daresay you'd
sooner it was the Gotobeds' and Godsave's than your
own.'

'There's sense in that,' Sir Tobias agreed. 'Except for
Godsave.' He gave me yet another hard look but went
on, 'You've been a damned fool, Trott,' and then
asked, 'So what d'you wish to do with him?'

'You'll have accommodation here? Then all I want is for you to keep him safe until the inquest. I'm afraid of his good nature and if we leave him free he'll very likely go running to the Gotobeds to warn 'em.'

Sir Tobias continued to look at me but nodded briefly and reached out to the bell. And when that excellent old gentleman his butler came in – Mr. Osgood it appeared – he gave his instructions, two more of the stablemen were fetched, and Nicholas Trott led away. The poor wretch was in a pitiable state, yet not without a kind of sullen anger which made it pretty certain that my stratagem was starting to work. But there were other matters to arrange yet.

When we were alone again Sir Tobias demanded, 'What of God's Name are you up to? Some other damned slim London trick? And this business of God-save . . .'

I was grieved to feel that he had such an ungenteel opinion of me, but interrupted firmly, 'I'm about a speedy conclusion, sir. For the best satisfaction of the righteous parties concerned and the upholdment of justice. And to that end I've yet several more requests to make; which I dare to hope you'll not refuse.'

'Begod,' he observed sourly. 'I'm coming to expect anything of you by now. What else d'you want?'

'I shall ask you first to have your men release Nicholas Trott at precisely ten o'clock tonight,' I said and, before Sir Tobias could recover from his surprise, added with a certain sourness myself, 'they may tell him that I am now proved a bullfrog in earnest, and you are satisfied there's no case against him.'

That shot took him fair and square, but he only raised his eyebrows to it. 'I've no objection,' he answered, 'though it sounds addle pated to me. And next?'

'It's a presumption, sir, and no doubt there are nice points of gentility to be observed. But I'd take it as an honour if you and my lady would sup with me at the King's Head tonight.' For the moment I thought he was about to laugh in my face and added, 'I repeat, sir, an honour. And I shall put myself out to entertain her with some light amusing anecdotes of St. James's Court and Kew House.'

'Her ladyship has a mind of her own. So if she will not come?'

'It will disarrange my plans. And your coroner might well have his jury bring a verdict against God-save tomorrow. In which case it will go hard with them who are sheltering him. For in declaring that he cannot have murdered my lord because they know where he was, they will admit to conniving at a highway robbery.'

'So you think Godsave is your highwayman?'

'Yes, sir. For certain he is.'

He mused on that, studying his hands folded on the desk, and then said, 'I don't see what difference my lady's supping at the King's Head will make.'

'There could be sundry doings at Hartingfield which no lady should be asked to witness. Moreover her absence will leave a certain freedom, as it were, for such doings to take place.'

'Very well,' he agreed at last. 'I can't answer for it but I'll send a messenger to Hartingfield directly. I assume you'll be taking some part in this?'

'The most active,' I assured him. 'I shall excuse myself from your company at about half gone nine and go to Hartingfield. And I'll be obliged if you'll have two or three of your good fellows attend to come with me, as I might need 'em to make several arrests. That being done I shall return to the King's Head in an hour or so to lay the whole matter before you and her ladyship and finish it.'

He regarded me somewhat quizzically for a time before asking, 'And that's all?'

'Not quite all,' I confessed. 'I'd take it as a particular favour if my lady would give permission for me to search Hartingfield if need be.'

This time he stared at me in open amazement, then slapped his hand down flat on the desk and cried, 'No, by God, that goes past impudence.' I did not answer and he demanded, 'What d'you fancy you'll find? Thomas Godsave?'

'No, sir,' I answered. 'I'm satisfied he's not there. What I'm looking for – and I mean to find it – is the document my lord was writing shortly before his murder. His lordship's last will and testament leaving all of his property, such as it was, to Captain Roderick Medfield.' In fact I did not give the worth of a tinker's blessing whether our fine lady gave me permission to search or not; all I needed was to have her think I might do so. But I let Sir Tobias digest that for a minute and then concluded, 'You'll see the way of it, sir. If that document still exists, and I'm certain sure it does, it affects my lady's title to her own jewels. If we ever find 'em.'

He thought about that for a minute and said finally, 'Yes; I see the way of it. And you'll forgive me if I observe that I shall be thankful to see the back of you, Mr. Sturrock.'

'Not near as thankful,' I told him, 'as I shall be to see the back of Roehampton.'

So I made my exit in some state, attended to the

chaise by the excellent Mr. Osgood. On our way back to the King's Head I gave Master Maggsy particular instructions of how he was to keep himself out of sight but watch every detail of my lady's arrival that evening – most likely in Sir Tobias's own carriage – and all that might pass thereafter. And on arriving at the stables I put further instructions to the post boy concerning certain questions he was to ask around this afternoon; even to the expenditure of several quarts of ale to my account if that should prove necessary. Not that the answers to them were so important but, as I have remarked elsewhere, I am a man who likes to have all things clear.

All was now well in train and, giving notice to Landlord Backus of the distinguished guest he was to expect tonight, I retired to take my ease by the parlour fire and wait upon events.

X

With the girl Bet to wait upon us it was a fair enough evening though not so merry as the first with Sir Tobias, as the better sort of ladies ever set a restraining influence. Maggsy, being unsuitable for such company, was banished to the kitchen though full of some secret which he wished to whisper to me, while my lady herself was very civil. She had a neat and not unamusing tongue which Sir Tobias described as the Gallic Wit, whatever that may be, and professed herself charmed by some of my anecdotes concerning His Majesty; even, I think, repenting of her forwardness in calling me bullfrog. But at length the stern call of duty was heard and I left them sitting at their ease, with Bet in attendance for propriety, and went first to get my pistols and then to find my men.

After some thought to our tactics I had resolved to mortify myself and take the first part on horse so that we might approach Hartingfield secretly, and have the post boy and Maggsy bring the chaise to wait on me there later for the drive to Westleigh. So three of Sir Tobias's fellows and a hack I had selected myself from Backus were ready at the stables, and without too many words spoken we mounted and set off into the darkness. It was snowing again, but nothing much, a very proper night for this work, and we passed along the lanes avoiding that pestilential heath and meeting never another soul. With the snow muffling the sound of our horses we rode silently until we came to the empty lodge and dismounted; where, leaving one man to walk the animals out of sight, I gave the others their instructions and led the way down the drive, keeping to the shelter of the overgrown bushes.

The front of the house was dark save for a glimmer in the hall windows and, keeping my pistols under my capes, we made our way round the side and past the coach house into the stable yard. Here there was a light in the harness room and the sound of voices, Buckle's and Hack's, and one of the horses was restless in its stall; banging against the woodwork as if the awkward creature knew there were intruders about. Otherwise all was well, but I left one man posted in the warm shelter of an open muck shed to watch events from there and come after Trott when he appeared. Then after first trying the scullery door – which was locked fast, Mrs. Peascod doubtless looking to the good of her throat before the gallant riding of Master Buckle – I led the other on through the arch-way and out to the rear court. Seen through the veil of falling snow some of the garret windows were lighted too, so it was pretty sure that the kitchen servants was safe out of the way. But there was one more window glowing on the ground floor, as I had hoped and ex-pected. That would be the Gotobeds' parlour.

Their private entrance was close by and I rapped on this with the butt of one of my pistols to be rewarded by an exclamation from within and then, after another sharp knock, with footsteps in the passage. The door creaked open a crack on a chain and I could just discern Gotobed's whey face peering out, asking, 'Who's there; at this time of night?'

'The law,' I answered, very short. 'Open up, my man.' But still the rogue wavered and behind him in the passage madam came asking 'What is it, Mr. Goto-bed?' to which I said, 'If you know what's wise you'll open; for Nicholas Trott's at liberty and from all I hear bent on another murder or two.' They gave a death rattle gasp at that, with more whispering, and I was fast losing my patience when at last the door swung back to let me thrust in past them; Mrs. Gotobed now more like a chamber pot than ever and somewhat dis-coloured. Bringing my man in too, but leaving him there on guard as I did not wish him to hear what passed between us, I hustled the two of them back into their parlour.

They were doing themselves nicely, as is the way of butlers everywhere. As warm and comfortable a room as I'd seen in this miserable house, a good fire and a bottle of my lord's port lying snug in its cradle on the sideboard. Observing, 'I see you're making the most of your chances before Captain Roderick takes all,' I paused only to examine the seal on the bottle, noting it was the same brownish colour as that fragment of wax found under his lordship's thumb nail – so con-firming my own deductions – and then added, 'Let's have few words. I'm of no mood for 'em and we've much to do in a short time if you're to save yourselves.'

Taking the pistols from under my capes I laid them on the table; at which Gotobed let out another death rattle gasp while the woman's stays creaked little less than a sailor's hornpipe. I said, 'They're not meant for you; I wouldn't waste powder and shot,' and went on, 'I see you've got paper and quills there. So lay 'em out.' Madam still did not move, though the obligato stop-ped; but her poor wretch of a husband looked sidelong at her and then at me and I roared, 'Lay 'em out; if you don't, by God, I'll let Nicholas Trott murder the pair of you and then take him for it afterwards.' He fairly jumped to work then and I finished, 'Whichever of you's quickest, sit down and write.'

'I'll do no such thing,' madam answered.

'Ma'am,' I told her softly, 'look at it straight. I know all about you. Likewise I know that at your age you'd never last a week in irons on a transport ship. You,' I barked at Gotobed, 'get down and write.' This time he sank on to a chair and reached for one of the quills.

'Mr. Gotobed,' the woman observed, 'you're a poor worm.'

'A worm with sense,' I rejoined. But his hand was shaking so much that I cried, 'God's sake steady yourself; you'll come to no harm if you do as you're told. Or not much.' That seemed to settle him a bit and I started, 'As follows. "Given in the presence of Mr. Jeremy Sturrock of Bow Street by us", and set out your full names, both of 'em.' Then, watching him add 'William Gotobed and Joanna Gotobed', I went on, ' "A true account of the events of the night of December 18 and this we swear to." '

With the woman watching me like a graven stone and never a squeak from her stays now I continued, ' "At a little gone ten on this night we was called in to my lord's cabinet, where he desired us to witness a document he had been inscribing. This we perceived to be my lord's last will and testament, by which he bequeathed his entire possessions, goods and chattels to Captain Roderick Medfield. Having so witnessed this we retired to our parlour, where we discussed the matter in some alarm, as it would be a bad day for us when Captain Medfield came to Hartingfield as he would be most certain to turn us both away homeless. But we concluded it was no serious danger at the present; for my lord was likely to live for many years yet and, having no great love for Captain Medfield himself, was probable to change his mind before the fatal event.

' "A little after this there was a tapping at our parlour window and I (Mr. William Gotobed) went to the private entrance, where the man Nicholas Trott was disclosed. Trott was somewhat drunk and demanding a bottle of port, as we were in the way of giving him from time to time; he and the coachman, Buckle, being aware of certain defalcations and embezzlements of ours against my lord." ' The woman's stays let out a veritable chime of bells on that and Gotobed himself stopped writing, but I said, 'Keep on now; we're doing very well. "After discussion it was agreed to give the man this port to quieten him; but as he was coming from the wine cellar with Mr. Gotobed my lord appeared at the green baize door from the hall, having heard the noise, and demanded to know what was afoot. My lord, still of a choleric temper, then closed with Trott and tried to wrest the bottle away from him; upon which Trott, being by much the stronger man, raised it and struck my lord a sharp blow on the forehead."

'Was he stunned outright?' I demanded; adding, 'Come now, I know the most of it as you see.'

'He was a little hurt,' madam observed. 'And swore he'd have Trott's neck for it.'

'Very well,' I said. 'Continue, "Upon this my lord declared he would see Trott hanged, and Trott then attacked my lord with both hands about his throat." And did either of you try to part 'em?' I asked.

The woman cast a look at Gotobed that spoke as much as a hell fire preacher's sermon. 'I did. Mr.

174

Gotobed was fearful.'

I nodded and went on, ' "Mrs. Gotobed then strove to drag Trott away but was no match for his strength and when at last he was prevailed upon it was perceived my lord was already dead. Upon this we (Mr. and Mrs. Gotobed) proposed to rouse the house and give Trott in charge but Trott swore he would expose our own crimes if we so did, and it was concluded that the least harm would be done by carrying my lord back to his cabinet and so arranging matters there to look as if the murderer had broken in from outside. This Trott added to by leaving a knife which he had stolen or otherwise acquired from Thomas Godsave." '

As we reached that the stable clock struck ten slow strokes and I said, 'We don't have much time; Trott may well be here in twenty minutes or so. Did he go back to the harness room?'

'I made him go to bed,' the woman answered. 'Lest the other men should see by his manner there was something amiss.'

'And which of you thought of purloining and suppressing the will?' I enquired. 'Very likely with intent to gain some advantage from my lady?' Madam did not answer, but turned another of her speaking looks on Gotobed; and I asked, 'Did he, begod? I wouldn't have thought he had the spirit. So write that down too.' The man was weeping now and I went on impatiently, 'Set about it. "In conclusion Mr. Gotobed proposed we should remove and suppress my lord's will, that being likely to do us an injury as Captain Roderick Medfield would now take the property, and also we might gain some profit from my lady by holding it over her." ' I watched him writing that and finished, 'Now you'll put, "We swear this to be the whole truth by Almighty God", and both sign.'

So that was done – not without some pleasure that I had seen it all by the art and science of detection – and I announced, 'There's one more thing. I'll have that will.' Mrs. Gotobed stared at me like stone again and for a minute I thought she was going to dare me and be damned, but then she turned to a little writing box, unlocked it and tossed a folded paper on to the table. One look satisfied me and I bestowed it carefully in an inner pocket saying, 'I'll save you both if I can. You're more a fool than a rogue, Gotobed; and you, ma'am, I'm satisfied acted but to protect him. By tomorrow I'll have some story ready which you'll tell and stick to. Your coroner's a blockhead and he'll be satisfied enough with Nicholas Trott. But for now that brave fellow'll be here any minute. He'll come straight to you and I want to hear what he says. D'you understand?'

It took yet more precious time to get into Gotobed what I was after, though the woman saw it clear enough, and then taking the pistols with me I went out into the passage and called my man, telling him to see that the entrance was left unlocked. There was a night light burning on a little stand and this I snuffed out before leading the way into the hall, where I extinguished also the candles on the centre table. Then we took up our position in the darkness on this side of the baize door, having it nicely half open so that we could get through fast if need be. I will confess that I was by no means sure that Trott would come; but I thought he would and, as you will already have seen, I am very rarely wrong.

In the event we seemed scarcely to have settled ourselves before there was a sound of something fumbling at the outer door, and it opened to reveal a dark figure against the dim whiteness of the snow beyond. He stood there cursing and muttering that now the old dog was dead the Gotobeds might have dared a candle, and then came groping into the passage. In another moment he reached the parlour and seemed to thrust the door back with his foot, to stand revealed in the sudden light; which revealed also what he carried in his hand – an old-fashioned, short double-barrelled pistol. This I did not expect, and was of two minds to challenge him myself before he did a mischief, but I had set up all this to hear what he had to say and hear it I would; nor could I stir yet, for he made no move to enter the parlour and Mrs. Gotobed herself spoke first. 'Nicholas Trott,' she said, 'what do you want here? And what's that in your hand?'

I did not like the sound of his voice. The fellow had been stewing the better part of the day and now was in a rage of fear. He answered, 'We're all in this, and if I swing we'll all swing together.'

Gotobed babbled something which I did not catch, but madam was made of better stuff. 'What're you talking about?' she demanded. 'Lower that thing, my man, and be off.'

He took a step into the parlour saying, 'You knows well enough. You've been talking. And Sir Toby says there's naught against me; so I can get clear away. But I'd as soon see you quietened first; or I might as well hang for you as my lord.'

The fellow was crazed, which I had not reckoned on, and cocking my own pistols I stepped out from our hiding place motioning my man to keep behind me; in which he was quite willing. But even I was not fast enough, for the end came quicker than I expected.

Gotobed spoke up, pretty near as cracked as Trott himself by the sound of it. 'Then you shall hang,' he cried, 'for I can bear no more,' while the woman said, 'Gotobed, be quiet.' Yet he went on, 'We'll swear against you, Nicholas Trott, at any cost; to the murder of my lord and have done ...' And that last word was lost in the thunderous crash of the pistol.

Mrs. Gotobed called out even as I reached the door to view the awful scene. Gotobed himself was lying over the table, his blood already staining the few white sheets of paper left there, while Trott now held his pistol levelled on the woman, about to shoot her yet afraid; and in return she was daring him, white lipped, with the look you give a lower servant about some rude act. Yet spirit as she had – if you like that sort – she could not have lasted a minute longer had I not lifted my own weapons and said, 'Come, Nicholas Trott, I thought you was a sportsman. What a cowardly rascal, to kill old men and frighten women. Come out and fight one of your own size.'

He turned with a snarl, puzzled in his poor wits by seeing me there, and backing up the passage to draw him away from Mrs. Gotobed I taunted, 'Come out and face a man who's beat you once before today.' That was near enough the end of me for on the instant he fired, and had I not seen the swing of his weapon in time to drop on one knee I'd never have lived to tell this tale. As it was the ball ploughed a mess of plaster out of the wall; and at the same time I discharged the first of my pistols, not to kill the oaf but to confuse him. Nevertheless he was still of a reckless mood and he flung himself upon me regardless of my second armament.

I might have had him fairly then, but you cannot

hand a dead man over to justice and I wanted him alive; though quietened. Sir Toby's man was behind me and no help from him for the present, so I fired again over Trott's shoulder and at once brought my pistol barrel down a sharp crack on his head; when he returned a most unchristian jab with his own weapon which would have put my eye out had I waited for it. This I struck aside, landed another blow which sobered him and then, finding the ill mannered rascal unendurable, went in to finish the business with no great nicety. Nor is there any doubt I should have done, and without assistance, but that Sir Toby's groom somehow worked round us and got his forearm round the mad rogue's neck, half choking him; so we pulled him down, and to make sure of it I gave him a parting tap with the butt of a pistol for a final touch of opium. It was a most ungenteel encounter.

By this time the kitchen servants had come scrambling down to see what the noise was about, making a fine fearful squawking of women from the hall; while at the far end of the passage Sir Toby's other man with Buckle and Hack were all crowding in at the door. 'Let's have it quiet!' I roared, causing silence to fall, and then kicked Trott's old rusty pistol along the flagstones. 'Where did he get that?' I asked evilly. 'Was it you, Buckle? Did you give it to him?'

'God's truth, no,' the coachman answered in a hurry. 'That I swear to; we never knowed poor Nick was back here. That's Nick's own pistol, he kept it hid in the coach house,' while Sir Toby's man put in, 'That's true enough, sir; he were routing and cussing in the coach house for a minute or two before he come out again and saddled a hoss.'

'He won't ride far this night; nor any other,' I

observed. My temper was not improved then by that impudent rascal of a post boy appearing with Maggsy and crying, 'Well, for God's sake, has the wicked old gamecock been at it again?' I quelled him with a look and turned back into the parlour, where Mrs. Gotobed was still standing with a face of stone and the sorry remains of her husband lying across the table. 'Ma'am,' I said with a nice sympathy, 'It's a most unfortunate event.'

'He was a poor worm,' she answered. 'But mine. Please to leave me.'

'Such as they are, I'll send the women to you,' I volunteered. 'But there's one last word, even in your grief. You'll do best to forget the business of my lord's will. Give only what information is asked and I'll see no harm comes to you.'

She nodded briefly, not caring much, and I withdrew again to the passage to find Maggsy feasting his horrible eyes on the scene of battle. Him I cuffed to encourage better manners, then gave instructions to keep Trott safe until something more official could be done, told Mrs Peascod – now weeping copious floods – to attend Mrs. Gotobed, and finally took up Trott's old double-barrelled pistol and called Buckle aside.

'Buckle,' I said softly. 'I'll take your word you didn't give Trott this. But I could easy change my mind. So here's a word of advice. There's more in this business than meets the eye and you might do well to say you was mistaken about recognising your highwayman as Thomas Godsave. D'you understand?'

'I'll be damned if I do,' he answered. 'But I'll say what you like so long as I keeps out of trouble.'

'As is the habit of wise men everywhere,' I rejoined.

Calling Maggsy and the post boy we set out, for

there was no more I could do here now. I was some-what displeased with myself for letting Gotobed be shot in that careless manner, yet reflected that with Divine Providence on your side all things work out for the best and it was one tongue less to keep silent. Our next business was Westleigh House. But before we started I asked the post boy, 'Well now, did you have any good of your questions this afternoon? And not too much ale, I hope.'

'Easy,' he boasted. 'It was like you said. You'm a knowing un as well as a gamecock. That day Mistress Bet herself took a hack out of the stables and led it up to the heath; then coming back alone. After that she went again gone dark and returned with the hoss.'

'You've done well,' I said; though it was not all that important, except I like to have everything tidy. 'And you, Maggsy? I observed you itching to tell me some-thing when it would have been most untimely. What did you see as her ladyship arrived tonight?'

'Landlord Backus and Bouncing Bet met 'em,' he recited. 'Landlord Backus bowing and bobbing and saying they'd prepared a retiring room for my lady. And she asks where is you, to which Bet said you was safe in the parlour, and then ladyship took something out of the carriage covered with a cloak and they carried it away upstairs with 'em. Also,' he finished, 'I reckon that should be sixpence too, for I'd a got another walloping if they'd catched me watching 'em.'

'In the science of detection,' I told him, 'a good ob-servation is its own reward. Now let's be off to find Godsave and have this business done.'

There is no need to burden you with detail over this next part as you will have guessed already that Westleigh was the only place where Tom Godsave could be; and I was going to fetch him. Arriving there I told Mr. Osgood and Mrs. Peggit simply that they must deliver him to me for I knew he was there. There was no threats used, only my natural dignity and some discussion; but I assured them that I would take full responsibility to their master, Sir Tobias, and so in the end they produced the fellow. He was very much as I had expected. A frank and open face as little like any villainous highwayman as I'd ever seen, and for certain a fool with the women; by the natural engagingness of his character Tom Godsave was born to a worse and longer fate than the gallows. And for certain the odd man out in that fornicating nest of rogues at Hartingfield; it was little wonder her ladyship made use of him.

So we started back, with him sitting beside me in the chaise and young Maggsy complaining in the straw at our feet. He answered my questions readily enough, which only served to confirm what I already knew, but was otherwise resigned in spite of all my kindliness. 'I knowed it'd end this way,' he said, 'as soon as Coachman Buckle recognised me. We hadn't reckoned on that.'

'You're all a pack of amateur fools,' I told him. 'And what's worse you didn't reckon on me. But it's not ended yet. For now we've a fair comedy to play out to everybody's advantage, even yours. Though you're catching a Tartar in Mistress Bet. Between her and my lady you might live to wish yourself hanged in the end.'

A comedy it was. Back at the King's Head I scratched at the parlour door politely and Bet came to it. When she saw Godsave she opened her mouth to squawk but, ever liking a good theatrical entrance, I put my finger to my lips to silence her and advanced into the room, where Sir Tobias and my lady were sitting one to each side of the fire looking both very handsome; for the first time I had seen there was a real smile on her face. It was not long however before I wiped that off, and with some pleasure. Making my bow I announced, 'Your servant, ma'am. I've found your highwayman and he's come to pay his respects.'

You'd have thought I'd fired a pistol under their noses they were so startled, gazing past me to Godsave, but before either could speak I continued, 'And touching the matter of your jewels. If Mistress Bet will go to your retiring room and fetch down the case you brought from Hartingfield, I shall recover them as I promised.'

For a minute there was silence, before my lady whispered in a curious voice, 'My jewels? You'll recover them?'

'To be precise,' I answered, 'they must be placed in the custody of the law, and an end to playing catch as catch can with 'em. From Thomas Godsave to Sir Tobias at Westleigh; from Westleigh back to you after my lord's death, ma'am. And now here to the King's Head tonight when Sir Tobias warned you I was asking word to search Hartingfield. As an officer of Bow Street I now call on you to deliver those jewels up to me.'

'Tobee,' she demanded, 'what is this man talking about?' and broke into her own barbaric language – no doubt a stream of shocking imprecations – but returned to the civilised tongue to screech, 'In my country such an impudent rogue would have been flogged.'

'Aye, ma'am,' I answered, somewhat nettled. 'And you got a revolution on your hands for thanks,' adding, 'Sir Tobias; you'll do well to advise her ladyship how the law stands.'

'Louise,' he observed, 'you've got yourself into a most damnation mess. I warned you it was a hare brained scheme from the start.' Looking across at Bet, now busy casting sheep's eyes at Tom Godsave, he said, 'Bet; go fetch the jewel case.'

'Tobee,' my lady cried again, looking as piteous as a prima donna on the stage. 'Do you desert me too?'

Turning no very favourable glance at me he told her, 'I do not; but we've no choice,' and asked, 'Well sir, how did you tumble on to it? By your art and science of detection no doubt?'

Ignoring that thrust and fixing my lady with a stern gaze, which nevertheless had no effect in putting her down, I began, 'When Lord Hartingfield's letter came to Bow Street I observed at once that there were several curious circumstances. I could not believe that a simple country fellow should suddenly turn highwayman, and seize jewels to such value at his first foray. A few guineas I'll allow; but not that. I asked why such a precious cargo was entrusted in a coach without a guard. And finally, through my own sources in London, I learned before coming here that nothing was known of the robbery nor was this jewellery expected in any of the flash houses. A flash house,' I explained, 'being an establishment where stolen property is received and disposed of.'

Touching on Sir Tobias waiting for me here and the interest of Landlord Backus and Mistress Bet – though drawing a kindly veil over her own disgraceful efforts – I continued, 'The murder of my lord is another

184

matter. But concerning the highway robbery I found that the evidence of two prime witnesses did not agree. Buckle swore Godsave was carrying one pistol; my lady that he had two. And I noted how she was curiously unconcerned about those jewels; which she told me herself were the last of her family possessions. It was clear that her statement was at least in part fabrication; for how can any man sitting a horse with a pistol in each hand seize and make off with a jewel case?'

Her ladyship looked wickedness at me but I continued, 'There were other doubts and observations, and even an attempt to lead me off the scent by mention of Captain Roderick Medfield. But I could see only one conclusion. That my lady took the jewels to the house party at Alton – which his lordship could not prevent – to the sole end that Thomas Godsave should relieve her of 'em back here on Putney Heath. He was to give them over to Bet and return to Hartingfield with some story to account for not meeting the coach at Kingston, having beforehand released his own horse to make its way back to the Hartingfield stable and mounted another brought from the King's Head. The purpose of that being lest Buckle should recognise a Hartingfield animal. It was, if I may say so ma'am, a singularly ill planned business.'

Bet returned then with a blue leather case bearing a tooled coat of arms and crest on its side and, gentle but permitting no denial, I took it from her myself while her ladyship watched with sudden death on her face. Between her teeth she said, 'In effect you pretend that I steal my own jewels. But why should I?'

'I would guess because my lord was preparing to sell them,' I answered. 'The fact is that though by every human and moral right these jewels are yours, ma'am,

185

by English law they became the property of the late Lord Hartingfield on marriage; as they are now the property of the new lord, Captain Roderick, by deed of will. And I have my lord's last testament here to prove it. Answer me one question,' I said. 'Is it correct that when you married Lord Hartingfield you did so in haste, and no legal contract or settlement was drawn up?'

'It is,' she answered shortly.

'Then at the moment you became Lady Hartingfield every item of your property became my lord's; even the clothes you stood up in.'

'As I discovered to my cost,' she observed.

'I do not defend that law, ma'am. But I suggest that when a few months back you were about to leave my lord, to retire with Sir Tobias to his Scottish estate, you would not go without your jewels.' She did not answer and I continued, 'I would think Sir Tobias advised you to forget them, for Hartingfield could have made an ugly business of it. But they were the last relics of your family and this you refused to do. So you devised your stratagem. With or without Sir Tobias's connivance?'

'Now be damned, Sturrock,' Sir Tobias started, but my lady cried, 'Without, Mr. Bullfrog. Sir Tobee said it was a damnfool plan from the start. He had no part in it until the end.'

'If you must know,' Sir Tobias said, 'I was flat against. Indeed I thought the notion dropped. Until Godsave appeared at Westleigh that night saying that things were awry and Buckle had recognised him. I asked what else he'd expected but took him in for safety, and the jewels. And be damned, sir, I'd do the same again.'

'A sad conflict between your feeling as a friend and your duty as Justice of the Peace,' I observed. He shot me a hard look but I was unperturbed. Taking the several papers out of my pocket, the Gotobeds' confession, the will and my lady's proclamation of the reward, I said, 'Let us pass on to other matters,' recounted at length the dire happenings at Hartingfield that night and concluded, 'It will save words if you peruse this confession for yourselves.'

While they were about it I desired Bet to have my clerk bring in a pot of claret for me and a quart of ale for Thomas Godsave; a generosity prompted by the thought of one thousand guineas. By then Sir Tobias had finished reading and he said, 'You've played so many confounded slim tricks that I'm bound to ask; is this true?'

'In every particular, sir,' I answered warmly, 'and borne out by my own investigations. It proves also that our highway robbery had no part with the murder; though it was the direct cause of my lord making his last will and testament. By which,' I added, quoting from it, 'he leaves every item of his possessions to Captain Roderick Medfield; "Being certain of my own mind and hopeful to see it proved that my lady had some part or connivance in this theft, or at least acted with such lightness and carelessness as cannot be tolerated".'

There was a little silence until my lady cried, 'Be damned to Hartingfield's will. Those jewels are mine and despite every law in England I mean to have 'em.'

'That's a bold statement, ma'am,' I observed, 'for the law may not be denied.' But I looked down my nose piously as I have seen lawyers do when proposing some nice piece of diplomacy. 'Yet it may sometimes be accommodated.'

'What d'you mean?' Sir Tobias demanded.

'Our problem falls into three parts,' I mused. 'The provenance of a good highwayman, the quietening of vulgar tongues, and the stumbling block of my lord's will.'

'Well sir?' he asked. 'Another confounded slim trick?'

'The alternative is plain,' I replied. 'My lady charged with compounding a felony, Tom Godsave arrested and yourself accused of connivance. While Captain Roderick Medfield takes all.'

'And that I'll not allow,' her ladyship cried. 'Come now, Mr. Sturrock, take no account of Sir Tobee. What d'you propose?'

'Thoughts only, ma'am,' I told her. 'Merely random thoughts. But we have a convenient low fellow known as Windy Jack, who fell while trying conclusions with me. He's past mortal care or calumny now. So let us suppose that I received some light of genius – as I do from time to time – and thereby returned to search the hovel in which he was found. Let us fancy that I discovered the jewel case concealed there. By no means impossible. So we might have an excellent highwayman to the best content of all concerned and no harm to any.'

Sir Tobias gave one of his hard, short laughs but her ladyship said keenly, 'But what of Buckle? He'll swear against Thomas for spite.'

I smiled gently. 'Buckle might easily be brought to admit that in the darkness and confusion he could have been mistaken. And the other servants, for what little they know, will conclude that still tongues earn the best wages. Likewise Mrs. Gotobed. I shall tell the murder story, which will be the whole truth forgetting only her part, and she'll not deny it. Trott cannot read and therefore knows nothing of the will; and aught else he says will be taken merely as vile and spiteful slander.'

Her ladyship looked at me curiously. 'But the will, Mr. Sturrock? As you said, that's the stumbling block.'

'I can scarce do anything illegal,' I said. 'Yet Sir Tobias and I might retire to the tap to take a glass of brandy and a pipe. And I might easily leave these documents lying here. Ladies are notoriously nice about tidying papers away.' There was a silence again while they digested that with some admiration, and I looked down my nose like a lawyer once more and coughed delicately. 'There will be certain conditions.'

'So?' Sir Tobias said. 'We reach the nub of it. And what are they?'

'That Thomas Godsave and Bet Backus are to be well set up and properly looked after for as long as they may wish it.'

'That is already arranged,' my lady answered. 'Thomas is to be in charge of our stables and to train as a racing jockey if he desires. Bet shall be my maid.'

I bowed and continued, 'Second; you shall make Hartingfield over to Captain Roderick on condition that Mrs. Gotobed is retained there as housekeeper. I fancy that with Bonaparte setting Europe aflame the gallant captain will have little time for mischief in the next few years; so she'll be assured.'

'And that's easy enough,' she agreed. 'For I don't care if I never see the place again. Is that all?'

I said, 'One thousand guineas.'

My lady's eyes narrowed, for as I have observed

189

elsewhere these French women are damnation hard bargainers, but at last Sir Tobias let out one of his laughs again and announced, 'I'll wager you play a very fair hand of whist, Mr. Sturrock. Very well, sir. A draft on Mr. Thomas Coutt's bank?' I bowed once more and he added, 'It's a pleasure to do business with you.'

'Then,' her ladyship cried, 'you have my permission to retire, gentlemen.'

So it was concluded. We had a pipe and a glass of brandy apiece in the tap – where, my fame having now spread, I was the centre of all eyes – and then returned to the parlour. Here there was no sign of the papers, nor that there had ever been any, and we passed another hour or so in merry but genteel style; even rendering the last verse of that canting ballad for her ladyship, which much amused her.

'Oh, I wisht I was a bo'sun bold, or only a
        bombardier;
I'd build a boat and away I'd float
And straight to me true love steer.
And straight to me true love steer, my lads,
Where the dancing dolphins play;
And the whales and sharks are up to their larks
Ten thousand miles away.'

And now I've done. As I promised, a light entertaining tale; though still with certain useful instruction in the art and science of detection. I have taken pleasure in setting it down, while young Maggsy has derived some profit from the practice of our noble English language; and I may yet consider relating more of my remarkable adventures and observations if this present is well spoken of and my publisher treats me fair. But that I am told by others of the scribbling fraternity is in the extreme doubtful, since they are all born with faces of brass and hearts of flint. But we must pray for a happy outcome, and in so doing I now subscribe myself ever your obdt. servant, Jeremy Sturrock.

In final; if any lady or gentleman should be troubled by some small slight mystery of murder, purloinage or similar mischief which they desire resolved to the best advantage of all parties concerned, I am always to be reached through the Bow Street Police Office or at the Brown Bear Tavern. Though it should be noted that this last is not a suitable rendezvous for ladies of the more precise sort.